Alexei's blue eyes darkened and kindled as if a flame burned in their depths.

He took her hand gently and turned it over, drilling a finger in the center of her palm. "You do have me...for now."

Britt snatched her hand away and jumped up from the couch. Did he have to be so brutally honest? Was she asking for forever?

Although she wouldn't mind forever. She pressed a hand to her warm cheek. He'd seen it in her face.

Alexei appeared next to her, resting one hand on her hip. "I mean, I'm here for as long as you need me."

She cracked a smile. "Be careful making promises you can't keep, Russki."

His hand slid to her waist, and the kiss he pressed against her lips tasted of vodka and expensive cigars and an aching truth.

He whispered against her mouth, "I can't promise you anything more than tonight."

After she untangled her tongue from his, she whispered back, "I'm good with tonight."

SECURED BY THE SEAL

CAROL ERICSON

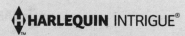

Recycling programs
for this product may
not exist in your area.

ISBN-13: 978-1-335-63897-7

Secured by the SEAL

Copyright © 2018 by Carol Ericson

Printed in U.S.A.

www.Harlequin.com

Carol Ericson is a bestselling, award-winning author of more than forty books. She has an eerie fascination for true-crime stories, a love of film noir and a weakness for reality TV, all of which fuel her imagination to create her own tales of murder, mayhem and mystery. To find out more about Carol and her current projects, please visit her website at www.carolericson.com, "where romance flirts with danger."

Books by Carol Ericson

Harlequin Intrigue

Red, White and Built

Locked, Loaded and SEALed
Alpha Bravo SEAL
Bullseye: SEAL
Point Blank SEAL
Secured by the SEAL

Target: Timberline

Single Father Sheriff
Sudden Second Chance
Army Ranger Redemption
In the Arms of the Enemy

Brothers in Arms: Retribution

Under Fire
The Pregnancy Plot
Navy SEAL Spy
Secret Agent Santa

Harlequin Intrigue Noir

Toxic

Visit the Author Profile page at Harlequin.com.

CAST OF CHARACTERS

Britt Jansen—Her sister missing under mysterious circumstances, Britt establishes a fake ID and gets a job at the strip club in Hollywood where her sister worked. She gets entangled in more than she bargained for and must join forces with a sexy navy SEAL who may or may not want the same things she does.

Alexei Ivanov—This navy SEAL sniper has a score to settle with the Russian mob who murdered his father, but his plans for revenge hit a snag when he agrees to help a fearless psychologist willing to stare down evil to find her sister.

Leanna Low—Britt's half sister is a flaky artist and recovered drug addict who lives life on the wild side, but this time she may have crossed the line.

Jerome Carter—The bartender at the strip club where Leanna worked knows more than he's telling; will he be willing to spill his guts?

Jessie Mack—A cocktail waitress who just might be following the same dangerous path as Britt's sister.

Tatyana Porizkova—A young woman from Russia who comes to the United States to live out her dreams, but may have found a nightmare instead.

Olav Belkin—A member of the Russian mob, he murdered Alexei's father and may now be involved in dealings with terrorists, giving Alexei even more reason to bring him down.

Sergei Belkin—Olav's only son and the manager of the strip club, Sergei knows how to keep his father's secrets and how to keep the women who work for him in line.

Ariel—The mysterious person running the Vlad Taskforce has no idea Alexei has gone after Belkin for his own reasons, but is willing to use Alexei's thirst for revenge to get more intel on Vlad.

Vlad—A sniper for the insurgents during the Gulf War has begun assembling an international terrorist network and has no qualms about using the Russian mob to further his agenda.

Prologue

The sun shimmered across the water of the Black Sea, but Alexei had his Dragunov pointed at the land, specifically a patch of emerald green lawn that rolled down to the beach. Alexei's lip curled at the deadly irony of training his Russian-made sniper rifle on… Russians.

The boat bobbed, and Alexei widened his stance, speaking into the mic clipped to his T-shirt. "We'd better get a signal here soon before the wind kicks up any more."

From another boat, his team leader's voice crackled. "We're waiting for one more member to show up—the most important one, an old-style gangster from the *Vory v Zakone*."

A muscle in Alexei's jaw jumped at the name of the gang that used to be the most feared and influential criminal organization in the old Soviet Union. New gangs had cropped up since the breakup of the Soviet Union, but the *Vory* would always be revered by the criminal world even as its relevance slipped away.

Slade, the team member sharing Alexei's boat, hunched forward slightly. "Why do we have to wait for him? We're not shooting any of the mob, right?"

"Nope." Alexei licked the salt spray from his lips. "But he's going to lead his terrorist friends into position on the lawn. I guess it's his house. He's their host."

Slade whistled between his teeth. "Who said crime didn't pay?"

"Not me." Alexei swept his scope along the large, rambling summer mansion perched at the edge of the sea in the Bulgarian Riviera.

Their team leader issued a command. "Get focused. We have movement."

Alexei tracked the new arrival through his scope. He focused and his heart slammed against the wall of his chest. A flood of adrenaline coursed through his body. He lined up the owner of the extravagant home in his crosshairs—the face older, puffier, but unmistakable.

He swore under his breath.

Slade shifted beside him. "You okay? You got your guy?"

Tracking his rifle from the old gangster to

the Chechen terrorist walking toward the sea, Alexei said, "I do now."

The countdown started. "Five, four, three, two…"

Alexei squeezed the trigger of his sniper rifle and dropped the target. His sniper teammates had hit the other terrorists at the same time, but, as Slade had pointed out earlier, the mobsters were off-limits. They'd set up the Chechens for the US military to take out.

Fighting terrorists sometimes led to strange bedfellows—despicable bedfellows.

Slade crouched on the deck of the boat and began to break down his rifle. He nudged Alexei, who was still hunched forward in his sniper posture. "You didn't get a clean shot on your target?"

"He's dead." Alexei swung his rifle from the lifeless body of the Chechen in the sand and zeroed in on the old *Vory v Zakone*, now laughing and smacking the back of one of his fellow gangsters, celebrating their safety.

Alexei's pulse ticked up a notch. His breath hitched in his throat. His trigger finger contracted a centimeter.

Slade hopped to his feet and jabbed Alexei's back. "Let's go, man."

Releasing a breath, Alexei lowered the Dragunov and rolled his shoulders.

You escaped this time, Belkin, but next time I have you in my sights you'll be a dead man.

Chapter One

Three Years Later

"Britt, I thought you were coming out here for a visit. I'm...in a bit of trouble. Call me."

Britt Jansen cut off Leanna's voice-mail message and stuffed the cell phone into her purse. Dragging the back of her hand across her nose, she blinked the tears away. She flipped down the car's visor and dabbed her pinkie finger at the edge of her heavily made-up eyes. She couldn't afford to lose this job before she started.

The Tattle-Tale Club was her only link to her missing sister.

She slid from her car, an old compact she'd bought from a private party when she got to LA. Although she'd parked outside the Tattle-Tale's lot, she didn't want to be tooling around in a rental car. She'd gone through too much trouble setting up a fake identity.

In the alley behind the club, she stepped around a transient's grocery basket to make her way to the back door beneath a red-and-black-striped awning. As she grabbed the handle of the metal door, the owner of the basket approached her.

"You got any spare change?"

"Sorry, no." She held up one hand as she yanked open the door and slipped into the back hallway of the club.

Irina Markov, the manager, had shown her the ropes yesterday, and Britt plucked her fresh time card from the rack and inserted it in the clock, stamping her arrival time. As she placed the card back in her slot, Irina bustled down the hallway, her dyed blond hair floating around her face.

"Right on time. Go introduce yourself to the bartender, Jerome Carter. We open in thirty minutes. Once the show starts, it'll get packed." Irina patted Britt on the back and then disappeared inside the owner's office—the owner, Sergei, who'd lied to the police about Leanna.

Britt squared her shoulders and blew out a breath. She could do this—she'd put herself through college working as a waitress.

The harder part would be getting into Sergei's office after hours, but she had a plan for that, too.

She strode up to the end of the bar and waved at the bartender setting up. "Hi, I'm Barbie Jones. This is my first night."

Jerome wiped his hands on the towel tucked into the waistband of his jeans and leaned forward, hand outstretched. "Nice to meet you, Barbie. Jerome."

"Good to meet you, too." She grasped Jerome's hand. "Do you need any help back there?"

He shoved a tray of small candles and cards printed with drink specials toward her. "If you could set up the cocktail tables with these, that'd be great."

Britt hoisted the tray and started depositing candles and cards at the tables closest to the stage.

Leanna had mentioned a nice bartender in her infrequent phone calls, but Britt had no intention of revealing herself to anyone—nice or not—until she could get a handle on the situation. Anyone in this club could be complicit in Leanna's disappearance.

The cops had just done a cursory survey of the employees and had come away satisfied with Sergei's explanation that Leanna—

or Lee, as she was known here—had quit to take off with a boyfriend. As flaky as Leanna was, there was no way she would've taken off like that without telling her big sister—and there was that voice-mail message.

As Britt moved to the second row of tables back from the stage, a woman approached her and tapped her on the shoulder.

"You really shouldn't put those candles on the tables ringing the stage." The woman, outfitted in the waitresses' uniform of short black skirt and white blouse, scrunched up her nose, shaking her head.

"Why?"

"Because when the show starts, those guys in the front row might start a fire when they reach for the dancers."

"Oh." Britt squeezed to the front line of tables and grabbed one of the candles. "Jerome didn't tell me that, but it makes sense."

The woman shrugged. "What does Jerome know? He's stuck behind the bar. I'm Jessie Mack, by the way."

"Hi, Jessie. I'm Barbie Jones."

Jessie narrowed her heavily lined eyes. "With a name like that, are you here to be a waitress or do you wanna be one of the dancers?"

"Oh, no, waitress only. Barbie's my real name, and I can't dance."

Jessie snorted. "If that's what you wanna call it."

"Are you here to waitress or dance?"

"I'm a waitress…for now, but I'm trying to get on the stage." She flicked her fingers at the stage. "You make more money shakin' your stuff, and I'm all about the dollar bills."

"Do you have to audition or something?" Britt transferred another candle from the front row to the second row of tables.

"Or something." Jessie grabbed two candles and two drink cards from the tray and placed them on the tables behind her. "There's a vacancy for sure. One of the dancers left recently, and I know Sergei wants to replace her."

Britt's heart took a tumble. Jessie couldn't be talking about Leanna. Her sister had assured her she was waitressing, not stripping, but then, Leanna didn't always tell the truth.

"Have you talked to Sergei about replacing her?"

"Have you met Sergei yet?"

"No. I interviewed with Irina." She'd wanted to meet Sergei, but Irina told her he interviewed the dancers only and left the cocktail waitresses to her.

"Yeah, that explains why you think it's so easy to talk to Sergei." Jessie put her finger to her lips as more women entered the bar. "Just stay on his good side…or stay out of his way altogether."

As the waitresses and the dancers flooded the bar, their chatter filled the air. Britt noted the heavy accents of some of the women and figured them for Russians since both Irina and Sergei were Russian, too.

When she found herself alone with Jessie again at the end of the bar minutes before opening, Britt asked, "Why do so many Russian women work here? Is it because of Sergei?"

"Sergei's father. He owns the place, along with a few others in the Valley. He has a Russian restaurant with a banquet hall in Van Nuys, so sometimes we work out there for events."

She touched Jessie's arm. "What you said before about auditioning for Sergei. What does that entail?"

"You mean what do you have to do for the audition?" Jessie rolled her eyes. "Use your imagination. That's why I haven't applied yet. I'm trying to get my courage up."

The bar opened for business, and Britt didn't have time for any more conversation or snooping. The customers kept her hopping with drink orders.

She bellied up to the bar for another order, reading off a slip of paper on her tray where she'd scribbled the drinks. As Jerome hustled to fill her order, Britt turned and wedged her elbows against the bar, watching the topless women undulate under colored lights.

"You want chance on stage?"

Britt jerked her head to the side, almost colliding with a dark-haired man with glittering eyes and a smirk on his lips.

She tucked her hair behind one ear. "God, no. I'm perfectly happy being a waitress. I can't even dance."

The man's eyes tracked down her body, and Britt craved a shower. "You have body of dancer. Maybe one day."

A chill pressed against her spine as Britt realized the identity of the man. "You must be Sergei. I'm Barbie, the new girl."

"Barbie, Barbie Doll." He touched his fingers to his forehead. "Welcome to Tattle-Tale."

He sauntered off toward the stage, his tight shirt clinging to his taut frame, and Britt sagged against the bar behind her, puffing out a short breath.

With a clenched jaw, Jerome placed the last bottle of beer on her tray. "First time meeting Sergei?"

"Yeah. He seems…okay."

Jerome's fingers tightened around the long neck of the beer bottle before releasing it. "Just don't get on his bad side."

"That's the second time tonight someone has warned me about one of Sergei's sides." She lifted the tray. "I can handle Sergei."

"That's what they all say." Jerome turned away without further explanation.

Britt couldn't stay out of Sergei's way if she hoped to discover why he'd lied about Leanna leaving her job and town with a boyfriend. Why would he say that? Unless that was what Leanna had told him.

She needed to get into Sergei's office, the sooner the better. She'd already discovered he left before closing time, so she'd have to figure out a way to stay behind after everyone left.

As Britt launched into the crowd of thirsty customers, Jessie grabbed her arm. "When you're done with those, can you hit a table in the front row at the end of the stage? Guy's been sitting there alone for a while, and I haven't had a chance to get to him."

"Sure. Which side?"

"On the left, facing the stage." Jessie jerked her thumb over her shoulder as she scurried to the bar.

Britt peered over her tray of drinks at a single man reclining in his chair—long legs stretched out in front of him, head tipped back, watching the woman on the pole. She mumbled under her breath, "Great—a weirdo by himself."

She scurried among her tables, delivering drinks and picking up a few tips. On her way to the lone guy up front, Britt stopped at a few tables along the way, scribbling drink orders on her pad. When she reached his table, she flicked a cocktail napkin down. "What can I get you?"

The man turned his head and pinned her with a gaze from a pair of the bluest eyes she'd ever seen. "Two shots of vodka and a glass of water, please."

"Hope you weren't waiting too long. The waitress at this station is really busy tonight, and she asked me to take care of you." Britt bit the inside of her cheek. She had no idea why she'd engaged this weirdo—maybe so she could stare into his eyes a minute or two longer.

He shrugged, his black leather jacket creaking with the movement. "I didn't notice."

Of course he didn't notice. He'd been too preoccupied ogling the topless dancer, who was still trying to get a tip out of him.

Without breaking eye contact with Britt,

he reached into his front pocket, withdrew a bill and tucked it into the dancer's G-string.

Britt felt a hot flush creeping up her throat and spun around before a customer could wonder why a cocktail waitress at a topless revue would be embarrassed by a common method of tipping.

She hightailed it back to the bar and smacked her order on the top. "I'm up, Jerome."

The antics of the dancers and the customers hadn't bothered her at all. As a therapist, she'd heard all kinds of stories from her clients and had learned to keep a straight face through all of it.

There had just been something so personal about what that particular customer had done—as if he wanted Britt to witness him touching the dancer in that intimate way.

She pushed her hair back from her face and fanned it with a napkin. She'd imagined it. The guy's appearance had just taken her by surprise, since she'd expected some dweeby loser to be going to topless bars by himself. That man still may be a dweeby loser, but he was one hot dweeb.

Jerome's dark face broke into a smile. "It does heat up in here pretty fast, and I'm not just talking about the girls."

"Busy place."

He tapped the last order on her list. "Is this a specific vodka on this order?"

"I forgot to ask, and he didn't say." She'd been too mesmerized by his eyes.

"Okay, I'll pour him the house brand. Ask next time, since Sergei stocks all the best vodkas. Even the house brand is decent."

"Will do. Thanks, Jerome." She picked up her tray and waded back into the mayhem. She delivered the drinks and then returned to her loner, still sprawled in his seat as if he hadn't moved one muscle.

She dipped beside his table. "Sorry I didn't ask you before, but is the house vodka okay?"

"It's fine." He shifted his body away from the stage, making a slight turn toward her. "How much?"

"Do you want to run a tab?"

"No." His long fingers were already peeling bills from a wad of cash.

"That's twelve dollars. The water's free." She giggled.

His lips, too lush for his lean face, quirked up at one corner, and he handed her a folded twenty. "Thanks."

As she reached for his change, he held up a hand. "Keep it…for the added comedy."

"Thanks." She backed away from his table and then spun around, nearly colliding with Jessie.

"Whoa." Jessie raised her tray of drinks above her shoulder.

"Sorry, just looking after your customer. He paid for his order already."

"Thanks, sweetie. Although from the looks of him, I'm sure you didn't mind waiting on him. I wouldn't." Jessie winked and squeezed past her.

Okay, so her reaction to the loner hadn't been completely out of left field—and Jessie hadn't even experienced his magnetism up close and personal.

She let Jessie handle him the rest of the night, although she tried to catch glimpses of him on her drink runs until he left. She had more important issues to deal with than men hitting up topless clubs on their own. The guy probably had a wife and three kids at home waiting for him.

After making two trips to the supply room, Britt figured out a plan for the evening. She could slip into the supply area instead of leaving for the night, wait for everyone else to take off and then search Sergei's office.

She'd already shoved a wad of chewing gum into the lock on the doorjamb of Sergei's office. Of course, if someone discovered that the door wouldn't latch completely, she'd have to figure out another way to get into his office. The plan sounded easy in her head until closing time approached and she got an attack of butterflies.

All the waitresses had to participate in closing down the bar. Irina had left at midnight, leaving Jerome in charge, which soothed Britt's nerves a little. If Jerome discovered her in the supply room, he might not even tell Sergei—it didn't seem like Jerome had much loyalty to Sergei.

After wiping her last table, Britt saw her opportunity. She tossed her dishcloth into a basket of dirty ones behind the bar. "Anything else, Jerome?"

"You can leave. You had a great first night."

"Thanks." Britt waved to a couple of the waitresses gossiping near the stage and turned down the hallway to the back of the club. She clocked out and then shoved open the back door. Before it closed, she tiptoed past the dressing room, where a few of the women were still chatting, and backed into the supply room. She crouched behind a stack of boxes.

About fifteen minutes later, the door to the supply room opened, and Britt held her breath. She didn't move one eyelash as the stacking and shuffling noises moved closer to her hiding place. It had to be Jerome finishing up, but even Jerome finding her hiding out would most likely end badly.

When the light went out and the door closed, Britt finally let out a long breath. She waited several more minutes until she heard that back door close for the last time.

Her muscles aching, Britt unfolded her body and peeked around the boxes. She crept forward and pressed her ear against the door. After the noise of the voices and the music, the silence pulsed against her eardrum.

Swallowing hard, she turned the door handle and stepped into the dark hallway. A few low lights from the bar area kept her from complete darkness, and she sidled along the wall to Sergei's office.

Biting her lip, she gave the door a bump with her hip. It didn't budge. She dug her feet into the carpeted floor and put a little more grit into it. The door popped open, and she grinned as she tapped the chewing gum wedged in the lock. The things you learned from clients, especially the juvenile delinquents mandated for therapy.

She took a step into the room, her fingers hovering over the light switch. She didn't want to announce her presence, but she couldn't see a thing.

She whipped out her phone and flicked on the light. Sergei's desk beckoned, and she accepted the lure, creeping around the back as if she wasn't the only inhabitant of the club. She tried the first drawer and gulped. She didn't have any tricks to break into a locked desk, especially inconspicuously. If she forced anything, Sergei would know someone had been snooping.

Gathering her hair in one hand, she leaned over the desk and shuffled through a few papers—orders for supplies and bills. Sergei didn't have a computer on his desk. He must take that home with him.

She put her hands on her hips and swiveled left and right, taking in the small office. Her gaze tripped over a filing cabinet, and she crouched in front of it, yanking on the handle. Locked.

What could be so private in a topless bar that everything had to be locked up like Fort Knox?

A sound from the back door had her blood running cold. Had Jerome forgotten something? A million stories started running through her brain in case he walked through that door. She wanted to change something in her employee file. She didn't have a place to live yet and figured she could crash here.

Her ears picked up movement in the hallway, a whispering sound. She dived beneath Sergei's desk, killing the light on her phone. Why had she left his office door ajar?

The floor beneath the carpet creaked, and Britt squeezed her eyes closed with the childish hope that if she didn't see him, he wouldn't see her.

The soft footsteps continued to the office, and she curled into herself, drawing her knees to her chest. Her stomach knotted and her lungs burned as she took tiny sips of air.

Her nostrils flared at the smell of leather and a faint odor of motor oil invading her space. Before her brain had time to fully process the smells, the chair she'd tried to pull back beneath the desk slowly eased away from her.

She wouldn't be yanked from a cowering position under this desk like some kind of thief. She rolled from beneath the desk and jumped to her feet. She gasped as her gaze locked with a pair of blue eyes.

The loner from the club stood before her... and he had a gun.

Chapter Two

Alexei clenched his jaw, stamping out the surprise from his face. He'd never expected that cute blonde American waitress to be hiding beneath Sergei's desk.

She obviously didn't have the same need to school the surprise from her face, and her big eyes got rounder and her jaw dropped.

He'd better be the one to gain control of this situation and go on the offensive. He tucked his weapon into the back of his waistband. "What are you doing in here?"

"I—I..." She ran a hand through her blond hair, and then she snapped her mouth closed and narrowed her eyes. "What are *you* doing here? At least I work here."

He couldn't bluff the previously giggly, apologetic waitress so easily, so he let his lashes fall half-mast over his eyes and growled, "How do you know I don't work here?"

She flinched, and he felt a stab of guilt. He'd laid it on too thick.

"I was just... I don't have a place to stay, and I thought I could crash at the bar for a few nights."

The back door of the club scraped open, and Alexei lunged for the office door and pulled it closed.

The waitress hissed at him. "It's not going to lock."

He put his finger to his lips as he took a step forward. Placing both hands on the waitress's shoulders, he pushed down, urging her back beneath the desk.

She scrambled for cover.

Alexei pulled out his weapon. Coiling his muscles, he flattened his body on the other side of the door and waited. If the door wouldn't lock, he'd better be ready for whoever came through it.

A man's footsteps thumped against the carpet and then scuffed on the wood floor in the bar area. The footsteps seemed to recede or had stopped altogether. Soft clinking noises carried down the hallway, and then a few minutes later the man's boots clumped on the wood again and were muffled by the carpet as he walked toward the office.

Alexei watched the door handle, his hand

wrapped around the barrel of his gun, ready to strike. The steps carried on. The back door opened and shut.

The woman beneath the desk sighed and whispered, "Is it safe to come out now?"

"For now, unless he comes back in."

She crawled from beneath the desk and brushed off her short black skirt as Alexei averted his gaze from the smooth expanse of her thigh.

Wedging her hands on her hips, she said, "You don't work here."

"Maybe not, but Sergei's not going to be happy when he finds out you were searching his office."

"You can't tell him that without revealing you broke into the club." She jutted out her chin and crossed her arms, daring him.

"An anonymous phone call would do the trick. He's a suspicious guy."

She tossed her head, flicking a swath of hair over her shoulder. "I won't tell on you if you don't tell on me. I don't care why you broke in here tonight, but I'm not going to be blamed if you decide to rob the place."

"That's where we differ." He raised one eyebrow. "I *do* care why you're here after hours, and don't give me that story about needing a place to stay. You didn't need to be in Sergei's office for that."

"I—I thought he might have a couch in here."

Alexei held up his hand. "Save it. You do realize we're both on camera, don't you?"

"Where?" The waitress widened her eyes and cranked her head back and forth. "How?"

"I'm not sure where all the cameras are, but he has one in that corner." He pointed to a camera perched on top of a tall bookshelf. "He probably has one at the back door, too."

"Then we're both in trouble if Sergei decides to review the footage." She twisted her fingers in front of her. "I *can't* lose this job."

Alexei tilted his head, his gaze sweeping the woman from head to toe. Why did she care so much about a job as a cocktail waitress in a dumpy topless bar in Hollywood—or did she care about being in this club specifically? If so, he needed to find out why.

"I have no intention of either of us being caught." Alexei pulled his phone from his pocket and accessed the club's video files that his friend at the CIA had hacked for him. A few taps later, he accessed the night's footage. He paused it as an African American man used a key to get through the back door.

"This is the guy who was just in here." He

held out the phone for the woman. "Do you recognize him?"

She nodded. "That's Jerome Carter, one of the bartenders. How did you get—"

"Never mind." Alexei tapped into a different camera and dragged his finger along the counter until Jerome appeared at the bar. "What do you think he's doing?"

Leaning in, her hair tickling the back of his hand, the waitress squinted at the display. "He's doing something behind the bar. The camera isn't picking it up."

"Do you think he's stealing something?" He jabbed his finger at the screen of his phone. "Looks like he's shoving something in his pocket, but that might be his phone."

"If Jerome has keys to the bar...and Sergei's office, I'm pretty sure he knows about the security cameras." She circled her finger above his phone. "I'm also pretty sure he doesn't have the ability to hack into the security footage. How—"

"You're right. Maybe he just forgot something. Has Sergei had any problems with Jerome in the past?"

"You're asking me?" Her voice squeaked as she drove a thumb into her chest. "This is my first night working here."

Alexei's pulse jumped. A cocktail waitress

snooping around her boss's office her first night on the job?

"Well, whatever Jerome was doing here, it's his lucky night. Sergei's not going to find out about it." He selected each of the four camera views and deleted the footage.

"Isn't Sergei going to be suspicious that he has no footage from tonight?"

"But he will." Alexei made a few more selections on his phone. "Just none showing any activity in the club after hours."

"Whew." She hugged the small purse hanging across her body. "Then I guess I'm glad I ran into you tonight. Thanks."

She made a move toward the door, and Alexei put his hand on her arm. "Not so fast. Since I saved your...behind, I want something from you in return."

A pink flush crept into her cheeks as she glanced at his fingers curled around her upper arm.

He released his hold and cleared his throat. "I want to know what you were doing here tonight. You already know I'm not going to rat you out to Sergei...or the police."

"Police?" She put a hand to her throat. "I wasn't here to steal."

"I believe you."

"Why should I tell you anything?"

"Because I hold all the cards."

She opened her mouth and then snapped it shut. A furrow formed between her eyebrows. "I'm not staying here another minute."

"I agree. It's Hollywood. There's a twenty-four-hour diner halfway down the block. Let's talk there."

Taking a step back, she reached for the doorknob behind her. "I'm not going anywhere with you. You could be some crazed killer or something."

"If I'd wanted to kill you, I would've done it already." He touched the gun in his waistband. "What reason would I have to kill you? As far as I can tell, we're on the same side."

"Side?" Her gaze flicked to his weapon and back to his face. "There are sides?"

"If you're worried, you drive over in your own car and I'll meet you there. Do you know the restaurant I'm talking about?"

"Half a block down on this side of the street." She dragged a keychain from her purse and dug some putty out of the lock on the doorjamb with a key.

He raised his eyebrows. "Is that how you got into the office?"

"Yep." She squeezed past him into the hallway, and her light perfume lingered beneath the smells of the club that still clung to her clothes and hair.

She turned suddenly, bumping his shoulder as he locked Sergei's office. "What would stop me from driving right home?"

"The fact that I can still call Sergei and tell him to keep an eye on his new waitress." He watched her green eyes darken to chips of glass. "And your own curiosity."

A pink flush washed into her cheeks. "You're mistaken. I don't care what you were doing here. I was just trying to find a quick place to bunk tonight."

"Really? You just asked me what would stop you from driving home." He touched the end of her pert nose with his finger. "If you're going to be in the espionage business, you're going to have to learn to lie better, *moya solnishka*."

FIFTEEN MINUTES LATER, Alexei pushed through the glass door of Mel's 24/7 Diner. The homeless guy in the corner nursing a cup of coffee didn't even look up. The couple at the counter, who looked as if they'd stumbled in after a bender on the Sunset Strip, gave him a quick glance and went back to stuffing their faces.

Only the cocktail waitress looked up and

eyed him as he approached her table. He'd need to get a name out of her before the end of the evening…and the truth. If she were actively working against Sergei, he liked her already. He also liked the way her green eyes glittered and changed color with every passing emotion. And that hair, like a mass of sunshine.

He slid into the vinyl booth across from her and extended his hand. "I'm Alexei Ivanov."

Those eyes widened, and her mouth formed an O. "You're Russian."

"I'm American, born and bred. My parents are Russian."

"Is that why you're sneaking around the club?"

"Yes and no."

"Are you KGB?" She put a hand over her mouth. "Is Sergei some kind of criminal?"

Alexei toyed with the edge of the plastic menu. She was figuring this out a lot faster than he wanted her to, and he still didn't know why she'd been hiding in Sergei's office.

He tapped the edge of the menu on the table. "The KGB doesn't exist anymore."

The coffee-shop waitress parked herself next to their table, raising her brows and the coffeepot. "What can I get you?"

Turning his coffee cup over, Alexei tipped his head across the table toward the other waitress.

"Umm." She ran her finger down the breakfast side of the menu. "Two eggs, scrambled, bacon and wheat toast...and coffee, please."

Alexei ordered some French toast, and when the waitress left, he hunched forward. "What's your name, and what were you doing in the club after hours?"

She searched his face as if trying to read signs there. "My name's Britt Jansen, but the club knows me as Barbie Jones."

His pulse jumped. She'd lied to the club about her identity. Anyone who could put one over on Sergei had his respect.

"And?" He circled his finger in the air.

Once the waitress had poured the coffee and left, Britt dumped three packets of cream into her cup and watched the milky swirls create a pattern on the surface of her coffee. "I'm looking for someone."

"At the club?"

"Yes—no." She picked up her cup with a trembling hand and slurped a sip. "I'm looking for someone who worked at the club but doesn't anymore."

"That doesn't make sense."

"I'm looking for someone who—" Britt leaned forward and whispered "—disappeared."

The one word, hissed at him in the nearly empty coffee shop by a woman clearly afraid, made the hair on the back of his neck stand up and quiver.

"You're looking for someone who worked at the Tattle-Tale, and you think the club holds some key to her disappearance?"

"I do, only because Sergei told the police that my…the woman quit, left LA with a boyfriend."

"Maybe she did. She's an adult, and people do quit jobs and move, sometimes without telling their friends."

Britt smacked the table, and his spoon jumped from the saucer. "She wasn't just a friend. She was my sister, and there's no way she would leave for parts unknown without telling me first. I tried to communicate that to the police, but they just shrugged their shoulders and said there was no foul play."

Alexei picked up his spoon and drew invisible patterns on the Formica tabletop. He had no doubt women in Sergei's employ vanished occasionally, but usually not American women with families who'd notice their absence.

"You called the LAPD when you couldn't reach your sister?"

Britt nodded, and her green eyes shimmered with unshed tears.

"What did they tell you?"

"First they told me I had to wait because she was an adult. When they did a welfare check at her apartment, they told me that while she had left some personal items at her place, it looked like clothes were missing and her car was gone. Then they talked to Sergei, and he claimed she'd told him after work one night that she was finished, leaving town with a boyfriend, and the cops told me it was over. They had no reason to investigate further."

"But you did. Is it just that she didn't tell you she was leaving? Are you and your sister close?"

"We…" Britt dragged a hand through her hair. "We weren't that close. We'd just gotten back in touch."

"So she could've left without telling you."

"French toast and eggs." The waitress delivered their food with a clatter of plates.

Britt waited until the waitress ambled back to the couple at the counter. "She could've, but I don't believe it. In the last voice mail she left me, she talked about being in trouble."

"What did the cops make of that?"

She lifted her shoulders and poked at her eggs. "My sister had some financial issues—unpaid bills, delinquent rent. That's what they interpreted as her trouble."

Alexei spread his hands. "You have to admit, the police make sense on this one."

"I know, and yet…"

"What?"

She patted a place right above her heart. "I know right here my sister needs me. I can feel it."

Alexei let out a breath and sawed into his French toast. Britt's sister was a flake who took off, leaving her sister to deal with her debts. Although Sergei was a dirtbag, he probably wasn't involved in the disappearance of Britt's sister—other things, but not this.

"What do you hope to discover skulking around Sergei's office?"

"I'm not sure. Personnel files, my sister's name somewhere."

"It's a dangerous game you're playing. Sergei is not someone to cross."

"I know. I sense that, too. I'm pretty good at reading people." She slumped back against the seat and broke a piece off the end of her bacon. "So, you don't believe he had anything to do with my sister or even that she's missing."

"I understand why you're worried, but I can see why the police declined to investigate."

"Now it's your turn, Alexei Ivanov."

"My turn?"

"Why did you break into the club, how did you erase that footage and how do you know Sergei?"

"I'm doing a sort of…investigation." Now that he'd determined Britt didn't have anything on Sergei, he regretted inviting her into his world.

"An investigation?" She crumbled more of her bacon between her fingertips, dropping it into her eggs. "Is that why you're so quick to side with the police? You're a cop?"

"Something like that." He had no intention now of telling Britt anything resembling the truth. She needed to get out of that club and go back to her life.

"After I gave you my life story, that's rather vague on your part."

"Just trying to protect you." He took one of her hands in his and felt her wild pulse beneath his thumb. "You should quit the job at the club and go home. Wait for your sister to call you. She'll probably contact you the next time she's in trouble or needs money."

Britt jerked her hand away from his, her bottom lip trembling.

"I'm sorry. I'm a jerk." That same guilt he'd felt before lanced his belly, and he wanted to press his thumb against her mouth to stop the quivering.

"You're just telling it like it is, and you're not wrong about Leanna." Britt sniffed and dabbed her nose with a napkin. Then she dragged her purse into her lap and pawed at the contents inside. "There is something else. Can you read Russian?"

"Yes."

"Maybe you can at least help me with this." She waved a Tattle-Tale cocktail napkin at him. "I found it with my sister's bills. I'm pretty sure she didn't learn Russian while working at the club."

He held out his hand, and she dropped the napkin. It fluttered and landed in his palm. He flattened the napkin on the table. "It's written in Cyrillic."

"Yeah, I have no clue."

Alexei ran his finger beneath the symbols, and when he reached the end of the note, he curled his fist around the napkin, crushing it.

"What's wrong? What does it say?"

"You were right, Britt. Your sister is in very big trouble…if she's even alive."

Chapter Three

A chill raced through her body, leaving a pebbling of goose bumps across her flesh. She swallowed hard and met the unflinching gaze across from her, as Alexei's blue eyes darkened to midnight.

She started to speak, her voice raspy. She cleared her throat and tried again. "What does the note say? Who wrote it?"

"A woman named Tatyana. She's a victim of…rape, of slavery."

"Slavery?" Britt wrapped her hands around her coffee cup, trying to warm them, but little heat remained in the lukewarm liquid. "Who? Does she name her rapist?"

Alexei released the crumpled napkin, and it fell to the table in a ball. "She doesn't name names, but I think it's clear who's behind the human trafficking."

Britt smoothed out the napkin on the table

and read the black-and-red lettering of the club's logo in the corner. "The Tattle-Tale Club? Sergei?"

"A good assumption."

"Why would my sister be in danger?" She flattened her hands against her belly to soothe the butterflies swirling inside. "D-do you think they tried something on her?"

"I think they're too smart to try to enslave an American with a family, but your sister must've known Tatyana. Maybe Tatyana was reaching out to her for help. If Sergei knew about the note, that would be enough to put Leanna in danger."

Britt chewed on her bottom lip. She and Leanna didn't have much family to speak of— just each other, and they'd done a poor job of having each other's backs up to now. *She'd* done a poor job.

"I don't understand." The strange characters of the note blurred before Britt's eyes, which were puddling with tears. "I work at the club of my own free will. I witnessed a bunch of women coming into work—some waitresses, some dancers—nobody forcing them."

Alexei drove his finger into the napkin on the table. "Maybe this Tatyana worked at a different place. They have more than one."

"They?"

"Sergei's family. They own a restaurant and banquet hall in Van Nuys. There could be other activity going on there."

"One of the other waitresses mentioned a banquet hall tonight."

Alexei's lean jaw tightened, and Britt could almost imagine smoke coming out of his ears from the anger that kindled in his eyes. He'd done his research. He knew these people. Maybe he could help her find Leanna.

"Is that why you were in the club? You're investigating human trafficking?"

He blinked once, his heavy lids shuttering the blue depths of his eyes. "No."

"But now that you know about this—" she poked at the napkin on the table between them "—you can bring charges against them. You can tell the police about my sister."

"Now that I know about this aspect of their operation, I can use it to further my own investigation. It's not a good idea to involve the police at this stage. That will just alert Sergei and his family and drive them further underground. We don't even know who or where Tatyana is."

Since she'd hit her own brick wall with the police, she wasn't anxious to return to them for help. She'd rather put her money on this blue-eyed stranger who seemed to understand the seriousness of her sister's predicament.

Drawing in a breath, she folded her hands on the table in front of her. "If you help me find my sister, because I refuse to believe she's dead, I'll help you."

He raised one eyebrow. "You'll help me?"

Her gaze dropped to his mouth—no twitching or smirking. At least he hadn't laughed at her. As she took in the soft sensuousness of his lips, at odds with the intensity of his face, she had a hard time dragging her gaze away from them.

"That's right." She blinked and swept her hair back from her face. "I'm inside the club, and I plan to stay there. I can find out who Tatyana is and how my sister knew her. I'll give you everything I have…and you'll return the favor by using your resources to look for Leanna."

Steepling his long fingers, he said, "You're putting yourself in danger by working at the Tattle-Tale. How do you know Sergei and Irina haven't already discovered your identity?"

"You *have* done your research. You know about Irina, too?"

He waved one hand. "Answer my question, Britt."

Alexei didn't have a detectable accent—

after all, he was a born-and-bred American—but he pronounced her name with a long *e* sound, like *Breet*. She liked it. She liked everything about him.

"For one thing, Irina doesn't know me as Britt Jansen. Like I told you before, I'm Barbie Jones from New York, nice and anonymous."

"And if they do a search for Leanna Jansen, are they going to find her sister, Britt, who looks a lot like their new waitress Barbie?"

"Leanna went by Lee, and we have different last names. She's Leanna Low."

"She's Chinese?"

"Half. After my mother split from my father, she…ah…played the field. Let's just say that the only reason she knew Leanna's father was Mr. Low was because of Leanna's features." Britt flicked her fingers in the air. "But that's another story."

"So the two of you don't look much alike?"

"Not to the casual observer. Believe me, Irina has made no connection between me and Lee-Low."

This time Alexei's lips did twitch. "Is that why your sister uses the nickname of Lee?"

"Yes." She tapped her phone and skimmed through several pictures with the tip of her finger. "Leanna has a quirky sense of humor and lives kind of a Bohemian lifestyle."

She spun her phone around on the table to face Alexei. "That's my sister. That's Lee-Low."

"They'll never guess you two are sisters, not by appearance, anyway." He studied Leanna's picture for a few seconds, running his finger down her sister's tattooed arm. Then he smacked the table next to the phone. "Delete this photo from your phone and any others you have of your sister."

Gasping, she scooped up her phone and held it to her heart. "I can't do that. I have so few pictures of her."

"Download them to your computer and then delete them. If someone at the club finds your phone, or snoops through it or even if you're showing them something else and they see any pictures of Lee, you've blown your cover."

"My cover?" She grabbed his hand. "You're going to take me up on my offer?"

He shrugged quickly. "I figure you're not going to leave that club just because I tell you to, so we might as well make this deal. I don't want you putting yourself in harm's way—no more skulking around. The cameras are going to catch you anyway. Don't ask any questions about Tatyana or Lee, but keep your eyes and ears open."

She was still in possession of his hand, so

she squeezed it. "I can do that. And you'll help me find my sister?"

"I will, and I'm going to start by searching through her belongings. Do you have them, or are they still in her apartment?" He drove the heel of his hand against his forehead. "Don't tell me you're staying in Lee's apartment."

"I'm not that stupid. I did pay her past-due rent and a few months in the future...just in case she comes back, but I rented myself a little bachelor in West Hollywood. I left Leanna's apartment as I found it, except for this." She pinched the Tattle-Tale napkin between two fingers and then stuffed it into her purse. "Like I said, it was with her bills that I took with me."

"Have you been back to her place since?"

"No."

"Anything else?" Their waitress had returned with a coffeepot and their check.

Alexei glanced at Britt, and she shook her head. "We're good, thanks."

As Britt ducked beneath the strap of her purse, she watched Alexei peel off a few bills from the same wad he'd used to tip the Russian dancer. His strong fingers moved with deftness and confidence, and for the first time since coming to LA to look for Leanna, Britt *was* good.

While Alexei had confirmed her worst fears about her sister, Britt now had someone on her side—a mysterious Russian American with acute knowledge and vast resources.

"Let's go, *moya solnishka*."

That was the second time he'd called her that. She had no idea what it meant and didn't want to know, but Alexei Ivanov could call her anything and she'd follow him anywhere.

As BRITT DROVE through her sister's seedy neighborhood looking for a parking spot, she continued to keep one eye on her rearview mirror. Nobody at the Tattle-Tale had any reason to follow her, but she didn't want to tempt fate. With that in mind, she drove around the block from her sister's place and parked in front of a different, although just as crummy, apartment building.

She exited her car and scanned the block, her gaze sweeping past an older couple walking a dog and a young Latino waiting for someone at the curb, his car idling and his music thumping through the open window.

She didn't even know what Alexei was driving. He'd walked her to her car in the diner's parking lot and watched as she drove away. Maybe he had a gadget to materialize and then disappear. She wouldn't put it past him after watching how he'd altered Sergei's security footage from his phone.

Hunching into her sweater against the gloomy late-June marine layer that had spread inland, Britt loped down the sidewalk. She turned the corner and made a beeline for Leanna's pink stucco apartment building.

She jogged up the steps to Leanna's place on the second floor and held her breath as she peered down the row of doors leading to about six apartments. She stopped midway at Leanna's door and inserted the key into the dead bolt first and then the door-handle lock.

Her heart skipped a beat at the whisper of movement behind her, and she spun around, her nose meeting Alexei's chest.

"Hurry, before someone sees us." He reached past her and pushed open the door, crowding her inside from behind.

She closed it and locked the dead bolt. Turning to face the room, she slipped the key into the pocket of her sweater.

"Is this how you left it?" Alexei took a turn around the small living room.

"Yes." Britt's gaze darted among Leanna's sparse furnishings, lingering on a row of oil paintings propped up against the wall. A dark piece with red swirls was still clipped to the easel in front of the window.

Alexei pointed to the painting. "Your sister was an artist?"

"Yes, and I'm pretty sure she wouldn't have left her work behind."

"Is it worth anything?" Alexei cocked his head to the side as if trying to make sense of the chaos on the canvas.

"They could be. She told me she sold a few pieces on the street at an art fair."

"Where did you find the bills with that note on the napkin?"

Britt crossed the room and rapped on the kitchen counter that doubled as a table. "Right here. There were three bills, and the napkin was stuffed inside one of the envelopes."

Alexei squeezed past her into the kitchen, his leather jacket brushing her arm. While the hot summer weather hadn't yet descended on Southern California, the jacket and his motor-cycle boots seemed like overkill—unless he rode a motorcycle.

He pulled open drawers and cabinets. "Looks like she took most of her kitchen stuff."

Britt snorted. "That's what the cops said even though I tried to tell them my sister wouldn't have had much of that stuff to take. It's not like she had a set of matching china to pack. Besides, I thought you believed my theory after finding Tatyana's note."

"Maybe she knew she was in danger and got out."

"That's what I've been hoping ever since you translated that note, but why wouldn't she contact me?"

"Fear? Doesn't want to involve you?"

"That would've been the old Leanna, but I made her promise me at the beginning of this year to call me if she needed anything."

Crossing his arms, he wedged his hip against the counter. "Why weren't you two close? Is it because you're half sisters?"

"We didn't grow up together." Britt traced the dingy grout lines on the tiled countertop. "My mother was a drug addict and lost custody of us when we were little. My father's family took me in, but they didn't want Leanna. She went to foster care."

"Your father?"

She shrugged her shoulders, hoping to convey everything, knowing it conveyed nothing at all. "Do you want to search the rest of the place?"

He pushed off the counter and returned to the living room in a few steps. He pulled the cushions off the couch and held up a quarter. "Payback for taking care of her bills and rent."

He tossed it to her, and she caught it in one

hand. "My sister doesn't have to reimburse me. I just want her back."

He continued to go through Leanna's belongings in the living room, flipping through her pieces of modern art. "These aren't half-bad. They convey a range of deep emotions—rage, terror, hopelessness."

"You see all that in those swishes of dark, heavy strokes of paint?"

"Must be my Russian heritage." He twisted his mouth into a smile—of sorts. "Anything else you can tell me about this room? Nothing missing from the last time you were here?"

"Not that I can tell. You think someone searched her place?"

"They may have done that before you or the police got here. It's a good thing she hid that note in her bills. I guess she was pretty sure nobody would want to look through those."

"Nobody but me." Britt caught her breath. "Maybe that's why she put the napkin with her gas bill. Leanna knew I'd grab all that stuff and take care of it for her. She put it someplace where she could be sure I'd find it."

"If Sergei's people never saw Tatyana's note, maybe they don't know anything about it. Although you can bet if Tatyana and Lee were close, they noticed."

Britt clasped her hands together. "Oh, God.

I hope Leanna got out of Dodge on her own, sensing danger. But why won't she call me?"

"Did the police ever ping her phone?"

"Turned off. My sister used cheap burner phones anyway. She was always calling me from a different number."

Alexei gave the living room a last look before heading to the back of the apartment. He poked his head into the empty bathroom, where a lone towel was hanging unevenly on a rack. "Anything in here?"

"No, and the police clung to that fact." She nudged him out of the way, liking the feel of his solid shoulder beneath her hands. She yanked open the medicine cabinet above the sink. "All cleared out. Nothing in the shower. As if some…kidnapper couldn't have swept all her toiletries into a plastic bag and hauled them out of here."

"Same story in the bedroom?" Alexei jerked his thumb over his shoulder at the final room in the dinky apartment, already making his way toward it.

"There are no suitcases." She followed him into Leanna's bedroom. "But honestly, I don't even know if Leanna had any suitcases."

He flung open the slatted closet doors, and the empty hangers swayed on the wooden rod.

Grabbing a handful of clothing on the other side, he pulled them forward for a closer look.

"These aren't all the clothes she had, right? I mean, most women—" he released the clothes and they rustled and whispered back into place "—have a lot more than this in their closets."

As she stood beside Alexei, relishing his shoulder wedged against hers, drinking in the way his dark stubble outlined his lean jaw, a horrible thought hit her right between the eyes. What if he had someone in his life? A wife? A girlfriend with a bunch of clothes?

"Sh-she wore a lot of different outfits with quirky accessories—hats, scarves." Britt tipped back her head and squinted at the shelf above the hangers. "I don't see any of that stuff here."

Alexei stepped back, and she was able to think again without all that masculinity crowding her. She didn't even know who or what Alexei Ivanov was. After her internet search for him this morning, she was pretty sure he wasn't a photographer living in Algeria or a boxer. He was probably FBI, and she planned to ask to see his badge or credentials or whatever before she traveled much further down this rabbit hole with him.

He sat on the edge of the bed and yanked

open the single nightstand drawer. He reached inside and held up his find, letting several connected foil packs of condoms unfold from his fingertips. "Would a woman take off with her boyfriend without these?"

"Exactly." The sight of Alexei brandishing an accordion of condoms did funny things to her insides, so she charged forward to prove otherwise, hovering over his shoulder to peek into her sister's drawer. She wished she hadn't.

"And those?" She jabbed her finger at the sex toys stuffed in the drawer. "A woman wouldn't take off with her boyfriend without packing *those*."

"I guess not." Alexei's eyebrows formed a V over his nose as he tilted his head to the side.

Britt nudged the drawer shut with her knee and brushed her hands together. "I think we pretty much put to rest the boyfriend story, although I'm hoping she hightailed it out of here on her own. Of course, that brings me back to the question of why she hasn't contacted me. She has to know I'd be worried."

"Did worrying you bother her before?" Alexei pushed up from the bed and whipped back the covers.

"Not really. Why are you doing that? What are you looking for?"

He flicked the covers back into place. "Bloodstains."

Britt sucked in a breath, and she plopped down on the edge of the bed. "If somebody did take Leanna, they grabbed her somewhere else. There was nothing out of place here when the manager let the police in. If there had been, the cops would've taken my concerns more seriously."

"Or they snatched her from this apartment and cleaned up after themselves." He dropped a heavy hand on her shoulder. "I'm sorry about that bloodstains comment. I forget sometimes I'm talking to Leanna's sister. I'm not used to working with…civilians."

"Who are you used to working with?" She looked up and locked eyes with him.

His hand tightened on her shoulder when the dead bolt clicked from the living room. He leaned toward her, his warm breath stirring her hair as he whispered in her ear, "It's someone with a key. Into the closet."

She froze, and Alexei had to grab her arm and pull her off the bed. He hustled her in front of him to the closet and propelled her inside. He closed the door, drawing a gun from his jacket pocket.

He always had it with him—and right now she couldn't be happier.

He gave her a gentle push to the back of the closet and arranged Leanna's clothes around her. As Britt inhaled her sister's signature musky perfume, she almost doubled over from the pain in her gut.

She must've emitted some scared-animal sound because Alexei put his finger to his lips. Then he crouched among the folds of Leanna's clothing and widened the space between two of the slats with his thumb and forefinger.

The front door slammed, and she jerked. She nestled in closer to Alexei's body, his warmth shoring her up. Her new position also gave her a view of Leanna's bedroom.

She took shallow breaths as she listened to shuffling noises from the other room. Could it be the apartment manager checking on something?

Heavy footsteps trudged down the short hallway, and a man burst into the bedroom.

Britt's fingers bit into the leather of Alexei's jacket when she recognized Jerome.

He flung himself across the bed and heaved out one terrible sob. "Lee, I'm so sorry."

ALEXEI DRILLED A knuckle into Britt's hip as he watched the bartender from last night thrash and moan on the bed. Just because Britt knew Jerome, there was no reason for her to reveal herself to him—and no reason at all for her to out Alexei.

But Britt kept as still as one of those shoes on the closet floor.

Jerome dragged a pillow over his face, wrapping his arms around it. His body convulsed with his sobs, and then, apparently spent, he knocked the pillow aside and stared at the ceiling.

Alexei's jaw ached from clenching his teeth, so he widened his mouth, shifting his lower jaw from side to side. He'd better relax. Who knew how long Jerome would gaze at the popcorn on the ceiling. He might even dissolve into another crying jag.

When Alexei realized he was still poking his knuckle into the curve of Britt's hip, he stretched out his fingers and smoothed them over the spot. He had to be more careful with Britt. He wasn't with his sniper teammates on this assignment. He kept making insensitive comments about Leanna and then would feel twenty shades of guilt as he watched the color drain from her face.

If he had to be stuck in a closet cheek to cheek with someone for hours, he preferred Britt to any one of his sniper teammates— even Slade, who smelled damned good most of the time.

After another five minutes of contemplation, Jerome rolled off the bed. He wiped his face with the hem of his T-shirt. Then he smoothed out the covers and plumped up the pillow before placing it back at the head of the bed.

He took a look around the room, and Britt pressed against Alexei's shoulder when Jerome's gaze lit on the closet.

Alexei coiled his already-tense muscles. If Jerome approached their hiding place, Alexei would have to take him down before he could identify him or Britt. He had no clue what Jerome's little performance meant, but Alexei wasn't going to take any chances—not with Britt's safety.

Jerome patted the sides of his short Afro and exited the room. A minute later the front door opened and closed, and the key scraped in the lock.

Still, Britt didn't move a muscle.

Alexei shifted his position. "He's gone."

Britt collapsed against the clothes. "What the hell was that all about? Do you think Jerome killed Leanna? Is that what he's sorry for?"

Pushing open the closet doors, Alexei took a deep breath. Even the stale air of the apartment trumped the cloying scent of perfume that overwhelmed him in the closet.

"I don't know." He waved a hand at the made-up bed. "Do you get the feeling this isn't his first trip to this apartment?"

"Oh, yeah. This is some kind of ritual for him. The act seemed to calm him, as if it satisfied his need to expunge his guilt."

Alexei's eyebrows shot up. "Looked like he was crying on the bed to me."

She shrugged as she ran her hands along her sister's clothing, as if straightening out the folds for her return. "I'm a psychologist in the real world, a marriage-family-child counselor."

"Which is why you were able to take off however much time you needed to do your sleuthing. And where do you practice? You never told me where you lived, although I'd assumed it wasn't LA."

"Charlotte, North Carolina—and you never told me a lot of things about yourself." She snapped the closet door closed.

He moved away from her and his desire to run his fingers through the soft strands of her hair. "Do you think the guilt Jerome was… expunging is a result of murder?"

"I don't know. Would a murderer want to be caught rolling around on his victim's bed, spreading his DNA? And what would his motive be? Leanna mentioned a bartender once or twice as being a nice guy—nothing more."

"Maybe that's your motive." Alexei moved into the living room and lifted the edge of the blind to survey the walkway in front of Leanna's front door. "All clear."

"You mean, he was hoping for something more than friendship and Leanna wanted to keep it platonic?"

"It happens." *Must happen to Britt all the time.*

"Then Leanna's disappearance didn't have anything to do with Sergei's family, the Tattle-Tale or Tatyana."

"You sound…disappointed."

"Disappointed that my sister was murdered by a love-struck bartender instead of Russian sex traffickers? I just want her home safe. I want to hear from her. I want to know she's okay." Britt's voice hitched on the last word, and she covered her face with both hands, her blond hair spilling over her wrists.

"I know. I say stupid things sometimes. I have no tact. The typical blunt Russian." Alexei rubbed a circle on her back. "But whatever happened to your sister, I'm going to help you figure it out."

She peeked at him through her fingers. "Even if it has nothing to do with your investigation?"

"Even then. What's Jerome's last name? I can start by checking him out."

"It's Carter. Jerome Carter." She swirled her finger in the air. "Are you going to look him up on your magic phone that will immediately spit out his name, rank and serial number?"

"Maybe." He took a turn around the room. "Let's get out of here before any more surprise visitors show up. Did we leave everything as we found it?"

"We didn't disturb anything, but I don't know if we can say the same about Jerome. What was he doing in here before he came into the bedroom? I heard some rustling noises like paper being shuffled around."

"Paper." His gaze darted around the room and stumbled over Leanna's easel. The dark, tumultuous painting now had a white corner. "Looks like he disturbed the painting on the easel."

In three steps he crossed the room to the window and lifted the corner of the heavy paper. "There's another painting beneath this one."

As he held the corners of the top painting, Britt reached over him and squeezed open the clips holding it to the easel. Alexei tugged the paper, and it peeled away from the easel, revealing another, much different piece of art beneath it.

A young woman from the waist up, nude, her arms crossed over her breasts, stared back at him with dark, fathomless eyes. Alexei's eye twitched, and his left hand curled into a fist.

"Oh, that's different from her usual."

"Do you see that?" He traced his finger along a tattoo on the underside of the woman's forearm. "A snake curled around the letter *B*."

"Not your typical hearts and butterflies."

"I know that tattoo."

"You do? What is it?"

"It's the sign of the Belkin crime family, and this woman is their slave. This is Tatyana."

Chapter Four

Britt ducked closer to the painting, her hand to her throat. "A tattoo? They tattoo the women who work for them?"

Alexei almost stopped himself from correcting Britt. Why did he always have to drag her onto the dark side where he resided? Then he shook his head. She never once asked him for protection, and if they were going to find out what happened to Leanna, she had to know the whole ugly truth.

"Maybe I wasn't clear before, Britt. Tatyana doesn't work for the Belkins. She's part of their sex network. They pay her in room and board and drugs."

"And those women at the Tattle-Tale?"

"The waitresses and dancers work and get paid just like you, but it wouldn't surprise me if Sergei was using the Tattle-Tale as a feeder system for the sex ring."

She released the clip at the top of the easel and tugged at the corner of the portrait. "I'm taking this with me. Tatyana and Leanna must've been friends. She probably told my sister about the trafficking."

"Putting Leanna's life in danger." Alexei refused to discuss whether or not he believed Britt's sister was already dead. He had no doubt the Belkins would murder Leanna for her knowledge, but she may have been able to slip away before they got their chance.

As to why Leanna hadn't contacted her older half sister and told her everything? Britt seemed to have romanticized her relationship with Leanna into something it clearly wasn't. If he wanted to give Leanna the benefit of the doubt, which he gave anyone, maybe she was protecting Britt. But disappearing without a trace was not the way to do it.

Britt knelt on the floor and rolled up the painting. "If Belkin's people did search Leanna's apartment, or...packed her things to make it look like she'd gone of her own free will, they missed this painting. There's no way they would've left this here for the police or anyone else to find, would they?"

"No, especially with that tattoo prominently displayed, but that means Jerome knows something, as well. He definitely looked at this painting before he came into the bedroom for his breakdown." He put out his hand to help her up.

"Thanks." She tucked the rolled paper under her arm. "I'm going to get to know Jerome better tonight."

"Is that a good idea?" Alexei scratched his jaw. "We don't know anything about him."

"Yet. You were going to use your resources to investigate him, right?"

"Yes."

"And while I'm at it, I'm going to get to know you better, too, Alexei Ivanov. I know you're not an artist or a boxer."

Of course Britt had checked him out. She wasn't stupid, or particularly trusting...despite her angelic looks and her halo of blond hair.

"You should know by now you can trust me, or Sergei would've fired you before your shift tonight."

"Oh, I'm pretty sure I can trust you, but can you trust me?"

He narrowed his eyes, noticing for the first time that Britt's pretty face included a stubborn chin. "What does that mean?"

"I offered to help you, too, but I have to know who you are and why you're investigating the Belkins if it's not the sex trafficking. And if you don't tell me—" she dragged

Leanna's keychain from the front pocket of her jeans and dangled it in front of his face "—I'm going to have to complain to Sergei about a suspicious man who comes to the club by himself and doesn't even watch the dancers."

He raised an eyebrow as humor and annoyance battled in his face. "You're kidding."

"I'm not kidding. You know everything about me and what I'm doing here, and you just keep tossing out these tantalizing hints. If we're gonna be a team, I don't want to be kept in the dark."

"You do realize that if you mention me to Sergei, I'll have to out you, too."

She snorted, her delicate nostrils flaring. "You wouldn't do that and put me in danger."

Alexei studied her face, his gaze moving from her dark green eyes to her resolute jawline. He'd prided himself on playing it close to the vest, but his protective instincts must've been on full display. "Pretty sure of yourself, huh?"

"Oh, yeah. I work with people every day, their deepest, darkest feelings all out there in the room between us."

"What if I told you you'd be compromising national security if you told Sergei about me?"

"I'd tell you that you'd better start talking."

As BRITT SAT across the dinner table from Alexei, she ripped a roll in half and dredged one piece in the small plate of olive oil between them.

She wouldn't really have exposed him to Sergei, and he probably knew that—at least she hoped he did. If Alexei had decided to tell her his secrets, he was doing so because he wanted to. The man across from her wouldn't allow himself to be forced into anything.

She held up the bread, dripping oil, and asked, "Why'd you choose this place for dinner?"

"Long Beach is far enough away from Hollywood to ensure we won't run into anyone from the club, close enough to get you into work on time, and I heard the Italian food was good here."

"You seem to be in a talkative mood, so I'd better strike while the iron is hot. Is Alexei Ivanov your real name?"

"Guilty." He held up one hand.

"Are you FBI, CIA, DEA?" She ticked off each acronym on her fingers. "I've run out."

"None of the above. I'm a US Navy SEAL sniper."

She widened her eyes. "That's not what I expected to hear."

"If it makes you feel better, I'm here under

the auspices of all those other agencies and more. The work I'm doing here is for a task force on terrorism."

Britt wiped her mouth on the napkin and took a gulp of water. This was heavier than she'd expected. "The Belkins are terrorists?"

"Not exactly." He flicked the side of his water glass with his fingernail and the ice tinkled. "We have reason to believe they're working with terrorists—it wouldn't be the first time."

"They're working with terrorists *and* they're sex traffickers. Anything else?"

"I'm sure there's more. The Belkins are a crime family. Back in Russia, criminals and terrorists are usually natural enemies. The majority of crime families are Russian, and the majority of terrorists in Russia are Chechen—no love lost there. But here?" He spread his hands.

"Anything goes if it's profitable?"

"Exactly." He tapped his head. "You're a smart woman, Britt. It's going to get you in trouble."

"Don't worry about me." She brushed some crumbs from her fingertips. "How do you hope to prove this link between the Belkin family and terrorists?"

"We have to catch them in the act—meetings, payments, exchanges. If the Belkins are smuggling women into the US to work in their clubs and then trafficking them, they might also be helping the terrorists get their people into the country. If the Belkins are dealing in arms, they might be supplying those weapons to the terrorists. We only have our suspicions at this point, no proof."

The waiter delivered their lasagna. "Anything else?"

They both declined, and when the waiter left, Britt pushed her plate aside and crossed her arms on the table. "And I suppose you can't just call the LAPD or the sheriff's department to raid the clubs."

"They keep everything legal on the surface. Those women at the clubs? They're just topless dancers, nothing illegal about that. If someone is paying them for sex, the police can bust them on pandering charges, but Sergei, or rather his father, is too smart to let that happen. The women they get over here from Russia are too afraid to come forward, or they're drugged. In a lot of cases, their families are at risk back home in Russia."

"Tatyana must've trusted Leanna enough to tell her what was going on."

"And put her in danger."

"Leanna probably encouraged Tatyana without realizing how serious it all was."

He aimed his fork at her food. "Are you going to eat that?"

"I ate too much bread." She hunched forward over her crossed arms. "If I can find some proof of the trafficking in the club, that'll help you, right?"

"You're not going to find proof of that. Don't even try, but if you can find out who Tatyana is and where she is now, that would help." He reached out and grabbed her wrist as she pulled her plate toward her. "Discreetly."

"I'm a therapist. I'm the definition of discretion."

He released her wrist. "I'm going to be at the club tonight."

"Do you think that's a good idea?" She jabbed at the thick layer of cheese smothering her lasagna, hoping that wasn't jealousy that just flared in her chest. "A single guy at a club like that—two nights in a row?"

"I have to start making contacts." He plunged his fork into his lasagna. "Don't tell me you don't have any lonely male clients. Going to strip clubs is not exactly a social event for some men."

"Yeah, I guess I have a few clients who frequent nudie clubs and hookers." *But none of them look like you.*

"Men in town for business. Newly divorced men. All types, I'm sure."

Her gaze darted to the third finger of his left hand and nothing had changed. He didn't even have a tan line there. "Has that ever been you?"

"Going to strip clubs by myself?"

"Newly divorced."

"Never married."

Nodding, she pressed her lips together to squash out her smile.

"Never wanted to get married—not with the job I have."

Now she didn't need to try. Her happiness at his first declaration evaporated after his second. "I'm pretty sure tons of military guys are married, even navy SEALs who are deployed. I know that for a fact since I volunteer to work with PTSD survivors."

"That's admirable." The customary tightness of his jaw relaxed, and his blue eyes almost sparkled. "I have a teammate, a friend, Miguel, who went through the wringer when he was captured by enemy forces. He's dealing with a lot of the ramifications of his imprisonment."

"Is he married?"

"Yeah, just got married. Has a son."

"I rest my case."

"You had a case? I know a lot of military men are married, but it's not for me."

If she had any appetite for her meal, she'd just lost it completely. "We'd better head back up north. I don't want to be late for my shift."

Ten minutes later, Britt stepped outside the restaurant and lifted her face to the sea-scented fog that had rolled in from the Pacific. She and Alexei had arrived separately again, and now she knew why as she watched him straddle a motorcycle.

After adjusting his helmet, he lifted his hand in goodbye and roared out of the parking lot. As she watched the taillight of his bike get sucked into the fog, she straightened her spine and marched to her car.

Whether Alexei Ivanov was marriage material or not was no concern of hers. She'd never met a man yet who wanted to stay. Why would Alexei be any different?

BRITT SMILED AT Jerome and then dropped her eyelashes, trying to hide the pity in her eyes. She didn't believe for a minute that Jerome had anything to do with Leanna's disappearance.

Apparently, Alexei didn't either since he'd

revealed at dinner that Jerome had been honorably discharged from the army and had never been in trouble with the law. They had no reason to suspect him...but Britt still wanted to know what the scene in Leanna's apartment meant.

Jerome swiped the bar with a cloth for about the tenth time since she'd been standing there and glanced over his shoulder at the back of the club. "Have you seen Sergei tonight?"

"No. Why?"

Jerome licked his lips. "Ah, just wanted to confirm some supply orders with him."

Britt shrugged. "I'm sure he'll come in later. Doesn't he usually?"

"Onto the floor of the club later, but he's typically in his office before the club opens." On his final swipe, Jerome knocked the condiment tray, and two maraschino cherries jumped from their container and rolled on the counter.

Plucking them up by their stems, Britt dangled them close to her lips. "Can't use these in the drinks now, right?"

"Knock yourself out."

She pulled the cherries off their stems with her teeth and then spun around to continue setting up the tables.

Jerome had better lose those jitters before

he talked to Sergei and aroused his suspicions. She wished she could assure Jerome that his after-hours foray into the club last night had been wiped clean from the video footage, but she couldn't do that without giving up Alexei.

Jessie was the first one in again, and she helped Britt with the setup.

As Britt handed Jessie a candle, she asked, "Have you gotten up the courage to ask Sergei for an audition yet?"

"As a matter of fact, I asked him last night since he seemed to be in such a good mood."

"And?"

"And I'm going to shake my stuff for him after closing time tonight."

Britt touched Jessie's arm. "Be careful."

"Really?" Jessie snorted. "I can handle a guy like Sergei. Besides, Irina's sticking around, too."

"That's good." Although she didn't trust Irina either, Britt squeezed Jessie's arm. Was she one of the Belkins? She'd forgotten to ask Alexei.

"What was the name of the dancer who quit, anyway?" Britt held her breath, expecting the worst. She hadn't wanted to ask before because she was afraid Leanna had lied to her once again about not stripping anymore.

"The dancer who quit? They come and go."

Jessie flicked her long fingernails in the air. "I think the last one who left was Tatyana or something Russian like that. Maybe Natalya. Is that Russian? I can't keep them straight."

Britt clenched her jaw to keep it from falling open. "I think it's Russian. Why did Tatyana quit?"

"Who knows? Left over four months ago. Scared little mouse who didn't belong on the stage." Jessie smoothed her skirt over her curvy hips. "You ready to have your socks knocked off, Sergei?"

Britt froze. She didn't have to turn around to know Sergei was right behind her. His spicy cologne invaded her nostrils, invaded her space.

How much of their conversation had he heard?

"I'm ready for socks to be knocked off, Jessie." He put his hand on Britt's shoulder and she jumped. "You ready to knock socks off, too?"

Britt plastered a smile on her face and twisted her head over her shoulder. "I think I already told you—I'm no dancer. I prefer to be on this side of the stage."

"Maybe you're right. Russians—" he snapped his fingers above his head and stomped his feet

"—are natural dancers. Most of our dancers here, Russian."

"The Tattle-Tale Club is hardly the Bolshoi." Britt placed her last candle on the table and felt Sergei's stillness behind her.

She turned to face him and a cold dread seeped into her flesh as she met his flat, dark eyes. Sergei didn't like to be mocked.

"I—I'm just kidding. The women I saw last night are quite good, and the guys loved them."

Sergei's thin lips stretched into a smile that didn't reach his fathomless eyes. "Tattle-Tale has only the best. Maybe not Bolshoi, but Bolshoi of topless dancers, eh?"

Jessie poked him in the chest. "And I'm gonna show you this American girl can out-dance any Russian chick. C'mon, Sergei. You've had a few Russian women in here who had absolutely no stage presence."

Britt's face ached from the fake smile and now a pain lanced her gut as she waited for Jessie to drop the other shoe.

"Ha! Who is that? All Tattle-Tale dancers beautiful girls."

"Sergei." Jerome broke into their circle, waving some receipts. "I need to talk to you about a couple of orders."

"Jerome is all business. That's what I like.

You two—" he wagged his finger between Britt and Jessie "—back to work."

Britt didn't breathe until she'd slammed the ladies' room door behind her. Hunching over the sink, she stared into the mirror. Had Sergei known she and Jessie had been talking about Tatyana? Had Jerome interrupted the conversation to stop it?

Jerome must know something about Tatyana. He'd seen Leanna's painting of the woman.

Maybe she and Jerome could pool their resources and help each other. He'd definitely interrupted that conversation just when Jessie was going to mention Tatyana, revealing that the two of them had been discussing her. She did not want to get on Sergei's radar as someone interested in Tatyana. Look where it had gotten Leanna.

The customers rolled into the club, repeat clicntcle and groups of men and some couples and some loners—including Alexei.

Jessie had his table again, but Britt would have to manage at least one visit before the night was over.

During a particularly dead set, Britt parked herself next to the bar on Jerome's end. She watched him retrieve a couple of bottles of beer from the fridge and then put her hand over his when he set them on her tray.

"Jerome, do you know where that dancer Tatyana went?"

He didn't even meet her eyes as he poured vodka into two shot glasses. "Leave it."

Ducking her head close to his, she whispered, "You do know something, don't you?"

He cinched her wrist, his fingers damp from the vodka bottle. "Are you looking for your sister?"

She jerked her hand away, knocking over a shot glass. "How did you know?"

"Lee showed me your picture." He whipped a towel from his waistband and mopped up the vodka on the tray. "You'd better hope she didn't show anyone else."

"Can you help me? We can help each other."

"Not here." His gaze darted to the left and right. "When the club closes, meet me in front of Rage. You know it? It's on Sunset."

"I'll find it."

Jerome replaced the vodka. "Keep moving."

Britt hoisted her tray and delivered the drinks. She'd have to get word to Alexei before he left.

He couldn't come with her. He wouldn't want Jerome to ID him as anything other than a devoted fan of topless dancers.

A short while later, Britt tapped Jessie on the shoulder. "You look busy, and I'm a little slow. Do you want me to take a couple of tables at the stage for you?"

"That would be great. I don't want to wear myself out before my big audition tonight." Jessie pointed to the other side of the stage from where Alexei was sitting. "You can take those few on that side."

"Will do." Britt headed to the opposite side. Let Jessie think she misunderstood her.

She waited on the table next to Alexei's and then sidled up next to his. She smiled and batted her lashes. "I'm meeting Jerome at some bar or club on Sunset after closing time."

He nodded. "No, you're not."

"He already knows who I am." She scribbled something on her notepad. "He knew right from the start. Leanna showed him my picture."

He swore under his breath. "You need to get out of here. Quit."

"That's not going to happen. He knows something, and he's willing to tell me." She tipped her head toward the stage. "Someone wants your attention."

He couldn't stop her without making a scene, so he hunched over the table and tipped the dancer.

Did he have to try to fit in so convincingly?

She hadn't even taken his drink order, but she'd seen the empty shot glasses on his table and the glass of water. She suspected that he dumped some of his vodka in the water glass to keep his head clear.

When she returned to the bar, Jerome waved her on to the other bartender. Was he afraid she'd start asking him more questions?

The next time she returned to Alexei's table, she included a note with *Rage* written on his cocktail napkin.

She placed the shot glass brimming with vodka on the napkin and smiled. "But don't show yourself. We're meeting in front, but I don't know if we're going inside. Do you know the place?"

"I don't, but I'll be there before you. Don't go anywhere with him."

"I won't." She took the cash he held out. "Enjoy the show—but not too much."

She hurried away from his table. Why had she said that? He was going to get the wrong impression of her, which was that she found him devastatingly attractive, and the only top-less woman she wanted him ogling was her.

Nope, that was the right impression, all right.

The next time she turned around from the

bar, Alexei was gone. Just as well. Maybe she'd see him at Rage.

She and Jerome avoided each other, too. In fact, this whole club was becoming a mine-field.

Closing time couldn't come soon enough.

As the club emptied out, Sergei emerged from his office and smacked the bar. "Jerome, you take off early tonight. Irina and I stay for audition, and we'll close up."

"Are you sure?" Jerome's eyebrows collided over his nose. "I don't have a problem clos-ing."

"I know you don't. We got this one."

Jerome shrugged but the crease remained across his forehead. He finished what he was doing and left the rest for Sergei.

As Britt brought up the last of the candles to the bar, Sergei smoothed his finger on a lock of her hair and then wrapped it around his finger.

"You want to stay and watch audition, Bar-bie Doll? Maybe you learn something."

Her breath hitched in her throat, but she managed to turn her lips into a smile. "No, thanks. I'll leave the dancing to Jessie."

She inclined her head to escape.

His grip tightened on her hair for a split sec-ond, and then he released it. "Serve yourself."

"It's 'suit yourself.'" She smacked her pad of paper on top of the bar and wiggled her fingers at Jessie. "Good luck."

"Thanks, sweetie."

Britt slipped through the back door and leaned against it for a few seconds, taking deep breaths of garbage-scented air. She preferred it to the air in the club.

Something moved to her right, and she jumped.

The homeless guy from the day before held out his hand. "Any spare change?"

She dug a couple of bucks of her tip money from her purse and thrust them at him. "Here you go."

"Thank you, ma'am. I'm Calvin."

"Nice to meet you, Calvin. I'm Barbie. Take it easy out here."

"You, too."

She loped down the alleyway and hopped into her car. Maybe Jerome had information that Alexei could use, information he didn't know what to do with on his own.

Britt looked up the directions to Rage on her phone and joined a line of cars in the late-night traffic. From what she knew about this city, parking wouldn't be easy to find on the Strip even at this hour.

She drove around the block and then headed

down a side street, finally parallel parking in front of an apartment building. She squinted at the sign proclaiming permit parking only and shrugged. If she got a citation, she'd put it down to the price for Jerome's information.

Tugging at her short skirt, she strode down the sidewalk toward the lights and hubbub of Sunset Boulevard, her tennis shoes a welcome relief from the heels she wore on the job. She turned left at the corner and then ran to make the light to cross the street.

Halfway into the crosswalk, she spied Jerome leaning against Rage's exterior. A steady flow of pedestrians crisscrossed in front of him, most heading home after a night of partying but some still looking for action.

Was Rage still open? Did Jerome believe they could talk under cover of the noise and crowd inside? Alexei didn't want her going anywhere with Jerome, but they couldn't very well stand out on the sidewalk and discuss a Russian crime family—if Jerome even knew that was what he was dealing with.

She reached the other side of the street and walked toward Jerome, who'd shoved off the building. They made eye contact.

A bunch of people staggered out of the bar behind Jerome, hanging on each other and laughing. The surge of humanity moved toward him and engulfed him, one of the party even grabbing Jerome's hand to drag him along for the hilarity.

Jerome broke away from her and stumbled against a man coming up behind him. Jerome turned and jerked, as if exchanging words with the man.

Britt picked up her pace, the group from the bar now impeding her progress. Somebody screamed, and Britt pushed past the last woman in the group, her heart pounding out of her chest.

When she had a clear view of Jerome again, he was on his knees, clutching his midsection. A rush of adrenaline shot through Britt, and she careered forward on wobbly legs.

Someone else screamed, and by the time Britt reached Jerome, he had fallen on his side, blood soaking the front of his shirt.

Britt dropped to her knees, pressing her hands against Jerome's tattered, bloody shirt. "Call 911. Somebody call 911."

She leaned forward, her nose almost touching Jerome's. "Who stabbed you?"

He parted his lips, and a trickle of blood and foam ran into his ear. "I loved her. I loved Lee. They killed her."

Chapter Five

"Walk past him, walk past him, walk past him." Alexei murmured the words like an incantation, but his spell failed.

He watched through narrowed eyes as Britt rushed to the fallen man and crouched beside him. The crowd around the victim ebbed and flowed—some scrambling away from the mayhem, and others circling in morbid fascination. A siren wailed somewhere in the distance, but too close for comfort or, at least, Britt's safety.

Alexei righted his bike and kicked up the stand with his boot. Traffic on the Strip had slowed to a crawl—a combination of the bars closing and the commotion on the sidewalk outside of Rage.

He edged his motorcycle into the traffic and then pulled an illegal U-turn in the middle of the street. He rolled to a stop in front of the red curb and yelled, "Britt! Britt!"

She whipped her head around, her face a pale oval, her arms elbow-deep in Jerome's blood.

"Get away from him now. Get on the bike."

Britt was no longer the only person kneeling beside Jerome. A man had ripped off his shirt and had it bunched against Jerome's stomach. A woman stood on the curb waving her arms. The sirens' blare sounded closer.

Alexei got ready to park his bike and haul Britt away from the scene if necessary, but she staggered to her feet. She spun around, wiping her hands on her skirt. With jerky movements, she made her way to the curb just as the first emergency vehicle pulled to a stop behind his bike.

"Climb on the back and hold on. I'll give you my helmet in a minute." He dipped the bike to one side, and as soon as he felt Britt's arms around his waist, he gunned it.

He turned right off Sunset and headed for the hills—literally. The Hollywood Hills climbed up above the noise and madness of the street, and Alexei kept going until he reached an unpaved road that circled around the property of one of the big houses.

He cut the engine and pulled off his helmet. "Are you okay? You looked ready to faint back there."

"I—I'm fine. There was so much blood from his chest to his abdomen."

"Stabbed." Alexei climbed off the bike and held out his arm to support Britt. "Did they kill him?"

"He was still alive when I reached him. Then he lost consciousness. I don't know if he died or not." She covered her face with one bloodstained hand.

"Hop off. There's a place to sit on the log here. I don't think the homeowners will mind too much…as long as they don't see or hear us." He placed the helmet on the ground and took her arm.

She slid from the back of the bike and collapsed on the log, a sparkling view of LA below wasted on them. "It was horrible. I didn't even see who did it."

"It was a man who came up behind him. He used the partygoers as a cover. He probably stole Jerome's wallet for good measure to make it look like a robbery." He sat beside her on the log.

She choked. "Did he walk past me?"

"No. He ran into the street after he stabbed Jerome, dodging cars and ducking between them. I lost sight of him, and I think he may have gotten into a car that was part of the line of traffic on the street." He rubbed her back, feeling the ripples of fear still coursing through her body. "That's a good thing. He didn't know Jerome was meeting you. Didn't see you."

"How did they know he was there at that particular time?"

"Sergei probably had him followed from the Tattle-Tale. I'm sorry they attacked Jerome, but I'm glad you weren't with him."

"Do you think we can find out where the ambulance took him and check up on him?"

"We probably won't need to do that. A stabbing in the middle of the Sunset Strip? Even if it goes down as a street mugging, that's going to be news." He tucked a lock of hair behind Britt's ear. *Solnishka.*

"God, the blood." She rubbed her palms against her skirt. "I don't know how he could've survived that."

"I'm sorry you had to see it. It's the stuff of nightmares."

"He loved her, you know." A tear dropped from her lashes and rolled down her face.

"Your sister? Jerome spoke to you before he passed out?"

She dipped her head and more tears dripped

off the end of her jaw. "Yes. He told me he loved Lee. He told me something else, as well."

Alexei wedged a knuckle beneath her chin and tilted her head. "What did he say?"

"He told me they killed... Tatyana. That's why Leanna was so scared. She knew what they'd done."

Not a surprise, but why kill a woman about to make some money for you?

"I suppose he didn't say why Tatyana was murdered, did he? You weren't by his side that long before that man joined you, the one who took off his shirt." He cupped Britt's face with one hand, his fingers nestling in her hair.

"He didn't say. He told me he loved Lee and that they killed her. I thought he meant they killed Lee, but when I asked him, he said it was Tatyana they killed. I asked him if he knew what happened to Lee, but he lost consciousness at that point."

"Maybe he'll make it." Alexei didn't have much confidence Jerome would survive that attack. Sergei's guy would've made sure of that.

Britt pinned her hands between her bouncing knees. "Why do you think Sergei had Jerome killed? Do you think he knew about him and Lee?"

"If he did, he would've made a move on Jerome earlier. You said your sister's been missing a month?"

"Over a month." She hunched her shoulders. "Do you think Sergei heard me and Jerome or maybe saw us talking on camera?"

"Sergei would've had his guy wait for you, too. It must be something else Jerome did to set off Sergei's suspicions. I wonder what Jerome was doing in the club last night after hours."

"I think Jerome was worried that Sergei may have seen him on the footage from the night before because he seemed nervous when Sergei told him to leave early."

"Turns out Jerome had good reason to be nervous." He put his arm around Britt and drew her close. "I'll get you back to your car."

She grabbed his jacket in her fist. "Alexei, I'm...scared. I don't want to go back to my place tonight, not alone, anyway. Can you follow me home?"

"What if someone's watching your place?" He held up a hand when she gasped. "I'm not saying you're under their surveillance, but they just attacked Jerome, and you were ten feet down the sidewalk from him."

"I hope his attacker didn't recognize me." She folded her arms across her stomach.

He didn't want to send Britt back to her apartment by herself, but he didn't want to risk being seen with her if someone was watching her place. He had a solution that made perfect sense.

"Why don't you come to my hotel with me tonight? Nobody's going to be watching me, and nobody followed us up here."

"Wh-where are you staying?"

"Beverly Hills."

"Must be nice."

"Let's just say I'm setting up a certain persona—in order to make contact with the Belkins."

"Like some wealthy Russian businessman or something?"

"Something like that."

Her shoulders slumped forward as if she'd been holding her breath. "I appreciate the invitation, if it's not too much trouble for you to put me up in your hotel room."

"Not at all."

The only trouble for him would be keeping his hands to himself.

ALEXEI PUSHED OPEN the door of his room, and Britt tripped across the threshold with her mouth open. "This isn't a room. It's a suite."

"Yeah, I think all the rooms on this floor are suites. Feel free to make yourself at home."

He let the door slam behind him, and Britt jumped.

"I'm sorry. You're still on edge."

She shrugged out of his leather jacket, once more inhaling the scent that had made her feel safe as she clung to him on his motorcycle, and hung it on the back of a white upholstered chair.

Spreading her arms, she said, "I suppose it doesn't help that I look and feel like a wreck. It's a good thing you have a bike that you were able to park close to a side door. I don't think the doorman would've let me in looking like this."

"You look like that—" he sketched lines in the air with his finger "—because you came to a man's aid. Having said that, you do have blood on your skirt, blood smears on your blouse, and that helmet didn't do your hair any favors."

She put a hand to her head. "I'm almost afraid to look in the mirror."

"This hotel supplies plenty of big fluffy towels and so many toiletries in there I don't even know what they are." He waved his hand toward the other room. "I pretty much limit myself to the shampoo and the soap, so knock yourself out."

"What about clothes?" She plucked her white blouse, stiff with Jerome's blood, out of the waistband of her skirt. "I can't exactly put these back on."

"In addition to those big fluffy towels, the hotel provides his and her bathrobes. I'm not a bathrobe kinda guy, so take your pick. That'll suffice for tonight at least."

She pointed to the door leading to the bedroom. "Through there?"

"Yeah, robe's in the closet." Alexei crossed the room to the writing table by the window. "While you're doing that, I'm going to try to find out some info on Jerome."

"I pray he makes it."

"Me, too."

Britt snapped the bedroom door behind her. Sagging against the wall, she covered her face with her hands. What if Sergei had the same man go after Leanna? When Jerome had said that they'd killed *her*, Britt had almost collapsed on top of him. Then he'd clarified that he meant Tatyana. Was that any better? Leanna had somehow become embroiled with Tatyana's problems and put her own life in danger.

That was so Leanna.

Buffeted by life's inconsistencies and cruelties, Leanna had a soft heart and always reached out to others in trouble. If she'd had half the compassion Leanna did, she'd have come to her sister's rescue a lot sooner.

Britt turned toward the mirrored closet and stumbled to a halt. She gagged at the blood smearing her clothes and even stuck in her hair, the night's terror crashing all around her again.

She toed off her shoes and yanked the skirt off over her hips. She practically ripped the buttons from her blouse in her haste to peel it from her body. She dropped it on top of the skirt and slid open the closet door.

Alexei's clothes rustled with the movement, and although she wanted nothing more than to run her hands through his things and press her face against the soft materials, she hung back. She'd wiped off most of Jerome's blood on her skirt, but the remains still stained her hands pink. She'd probably already gotten blood on his jacket when she'd climbed onto the back of his bike as the cops arrived.

Alexei had been right to get her out of there. She'd have a hard time explaining to Sergei why she'd been with Jerome after hours.

She yanked one of the terry-cloth robes from its hanger and trailed it on the floor behind her as she walked to the bathroom. She stood at the entrance to the bathroom, drinking in the black-and-white tiled floor, the step-down oval tub with Jacuzzi jets and the open shower with two showerheads facing each other. The whole setup gave her sinful ideas about the man in the other room, but she was here to heal and recover—not seduce.

She shimmied out of her underwear and snagged a towel neatly folded on a shelf beneath the vanity. As she draped it over the rack closest to the shower, she realized she had the option to heat the towel while she was showering. She flipped the switch on the warmer. She could get used to this.

She cranked on both showerheads for the hell of it and stepped between the dueling sprays.

Thank God the blood on her hands hadn't stained her flesh. It did leave a pink cast on the washcloth until she rinsed it out over and over.

She made generous use of the high-end products Alexei had dismissed, massaging the fragrant shampoo into her scalp. By the time she finished her shower, the knots between her shoulder blades had loosened and she'd stopped grinding her back teeth.

The towel rack worked, and she buried

her face in the warm terry cloth, wishing she could melt away and forget the feel of Jerome's slick blood between her fingers. She finished drying her body and then wrapped her hair in the towel.

The lotion the hotel stocked was good enough for a face moisturizer, and she slathered it on her cheeks and down her throat. She ran the hair dryer over her hair, snuggled into the robe and faced the mirror—almost a new woman. Her eyes still looked like they'd seen a ghost—several ghosts.

She huffed out a breath and picked up her damp towel from the floor. When she returned to the bedroom, she kept her eyes averted from the big bed in the center of the room and swept up her soiled clothing, wrapping the skirt and blouse in the towel and tossing the bundle in a corner of the bathroom.

When she strolled into the other room, she almost turned right around when she saw the midnight blue of Alexei's eyes turn black.

"I have some bad news, Britt."

"Is it Jerome?"

"He didn't make it."

She sank to the edge of the sofa, the rosy flush of her shower turning ice-cold. "Are you sure?"

He tapped his laptop. "An online news website is reporting it as a murder. Man knifed to death for his wallet."

"Oh my God. Why? Why did they have to kill him?"

"He knew too much, like your sister." He held up one finger. "Not that I'm suggesting your sister met the same fate."

"If she didn't, where is she? Why did the Belkins kill Tatyana? They had her over here, had her working at one of their clubs. They had her exactly where they wanted her, right? She even had the tattoo. Why would they go through all that trouble to groom her only to murder her?"

Alexei clasped the back of his neck with one hand and stared out the window. "I've been asking myself those same questions. Tatyana must've threatened to escape, or maybe they just pegged her as a risk when she started communicating with Leanna. She represented some kind of threat to them."

"Poor Jerome. He lost the woman he loved, and then he lost his life. What do you think he had to be sorry about? Why that scene at Leanna's?"

"He probably regretted not being able to protect Leanna, especially if she came to him for help." His profile at the window seemed carved in stone.

And then it hit her. A man like Alexei would move heaven and earth to protect someone he loved. To be loved with that kind of intensity would be overwhelming, but then, Alexei had proclaimed himself immune to any kind of lasting love.

It must be love of country that motivated him. The navy had taken him off military duty for this assignment. They tagged him as the man for the job for some reason.

"I'm not sure where we go from here. Where I go from here."

He turned from the window and perched on the edge of the sofa next to her, his knee banging against hers. "Back to Charlotte. Back to your clients, who need you. Back to safety."

"Leanna needs me. I was never there for her. I abandoned her when Mom died. I was her big sister, and I should've stayed with her."

"You can't blame yourself for that. It wasn't up to you. How old were you when your mother died?"

"Ten. Leanna was seven."

"At ten, you weren't going to be the one making the decision where you or your sister wound up. Your father's people made their choice."

"It was a bad choice."

"It was cruel." He traced the tip of his finger

along the curve of her ear. "But it's not your fault. Is that what you're doing in LA? You're trying to make it all up to Leanna?"

"I'm trying to find her. Who else but me?"

He shifted his hand to the back of her neck beneath her damp hair. "I'll do it. I'll try to find Leanna."

"You're here to find terrorists."

"One may lead me to the other."

She tipped back her head and studied the ceiling. "If I leave now, I'll feel like I'm giving up on my sister all over again."

"Don't make any decisions tonight. You've had a rough time."

"What did the news story say about Jerome?" She nodded toward his laptop, still open on the desk.

"The authorities don't know he's Jerome Carter yet. His killer took his wallet, I guess to make it look like a common street robbery. The story I read didn't give out much information—just that a man was knifed for his wallet and died of his injuries on the way to the hospital."

Britt curled her legs beneath her on the sofa. "Did the article mention any witnesses?"

"It didn't mention a mysterious blonde who was the first at the man's side and then disappeared, if that's what you're wondering. Did you get a good look at the guy? You could always phone in an anonymous tip."

"I didn't really see him. He came along at the tail end of a bunch of people coming out of Rage, but I don't think he was in the bar himself. Those people surged toward me, and I lost sight of Jerome for several seconds. When the people parted, I saw Jerome turn to face a man wearing a gray hoodie. Is that what others are saying to the police?"

"I didn't read any witness accounts. You can bet Sergei's guy is not going to be ID'd by anyone. The police aren't going to make any connection between Jerome and his place of work." Alexei stretched his arms over his head. "It's late. You should get some sleep. Take the bed in the other room."

"I don't want to kick you out of bed." She couldn't imagine any scenario where she'd kick Alexei out of bed. "I mean, kick you out of *your* bed...*the* bed."

He rescued her with a smile and patted the sofa. "This is fine for me. You're the one who had the traumatic night."

"Yeah." She splayed her hands in her lap, palms up. "I just washed the stains of a dead man's blood from these hands."

He traced the lines on her palm with his fingertip. "I wish I could read your palm and tell you everything was going to be okay, that you'll find Leanna and make amends."

"You've done a lot already." When he removed his finger from her palm, she rubbed her hands together, feeling the tingle of his touch. "I guess there's nothing left to do tonight but sleep."

He shot off the couch, all business. "I'll grab a pillow or two from the bed and a blanket from the closet. If you want something a little less bulky to sleep in, you can borrow one of my T-shirts."

"Okay, I might take you up on that." She uncurled her legs and walked to the bedroom. Pausing awkwardly at the door, she asked, "Do you need to get into the bathroom first?"

"I won't be long." He shut down his computer and breezed past her into the bedroom.

She sat on the edge of the bed as he grabbed a pillow and blanket and took them into the other room. Then he disappeared into the bathroom.

Once she heard the water running, she shed the robe and grabbed one of his T-shirts from the closet. She slipped it over her head and hugged the soft cotton around her nakedness. Even this small connection to Alexei made her feel safe.

Maybe he was right. She should quit the

job at the Tattle-Tale and leave it to the US government to take down the Belkins—not that some nameless, faceless bureaucrat would give a damn about Leanna or Tatyana. But Alexei did. He cared.

She snuggled between the sheets of the king-size bed and flicked on the TV for company—it would have to do.

Alexei emerged from the bathroom, the edges of his short dark hair flipping up with the dampness. He still had on his jeans and T-shirt, but he carried his motorcycle boots in one hand.

"You all set in here?"

"I'm going to fall asleep to the TV."

"I do the same thing. What are you watching?"

"An old comedy." She pointed the remote at the TV screen.

"I like that one, too." He hovered at the door. "Try to get a good night's sleep, Britt."

"You, too."

He pulled the door closed behind him, and she slumped against the pillows. Everything from his T-shirt to the bedsheets was freshly laundered, so she couldn't even revel in his masculine scent for company.

She traced over the lines of her palm as he had done, and her hand tingled in remembrance of his touch. If she left now, not only would she be giving up on Leanna but she'd also have to leave Alexei Ivanov forever.

And she wasn't ready to do that.

Chapter Six

The following morning, Britt peeked out of the bedroom door to find Alexei on his computer again. She tiptoed up behind him and peered over his shoulder. "Ariel? Is that your girlfriend?"

He jumped and slammed down the lid of his laptop. "Whoa. Sneaking up behind people like that is a good way to get your lights knocked out."

She blinked. "You mean you were ready to punch me in the face?"

"Instinct."

"Whew." She wiped her brow with the flick of her fingers. "Is that what they teach you in navy SEAL school?"

"Yeah, instinct."

He clearly had no intention of answering her question about Ariel. "Anything else in the news about Jerome?"

"His murder made the morning shows, and they identified him. Maybe he still had his phone, and they ID'd him that way or took his fingerprints, which would be on file with the army."

Britt snapped up the remote and turned on the TV. "Maybe Leanna will hear the news wherever she is, and it'll bring her out."

"Or drive her further underground."

She surfed the channels but had missed the local morning news shows, and a murder on the Sunset Strip hadn't made national news—yet.

Alexei opened his laptop again and presumably continued his communication with Ariel. "I'm going to order us some room service for breakfast, and then we'll take a car to your car. I don't want either of us riding on the bike without a helmet and risk getting pulled over. But first you need to get some clothes. You can't wear that skirt and blouse in the light of day."

"How am I going to go shopping?"

"If you didn't notice last night, this hotel has everything. There are a couple of clothing stores on the first level. Give me your size, and I'll pick up a dress for you—something simple so it won't matter if it's not a perfect fit."

"All right, but I'm going to have to go out this afternoon and buy another black skirt and white blouse to wear at the Tattle-Tale."

He twisted his head around. "So you decided to go back?"

"I sort of have to, at least for tonight's shift. How would it look if I quit or disappeared right after Jerome's murder?"

"What does it matter if you're on your way back to North Carolina?"

"That remains to be seen."

He lifted his shoulders. "I'm not going to tell you what to do, except to look at the breakfast menu so we can eat and get out of here."

And they did just that. Alexei showered while she waited for the food to arrive. Then they ate, and she showered while he went downstairs to buy her a dress.

He came back with a casual loose-fitting blue dress that hit her right above the knee.

She twirled in front of the mirror on the toes of her sneakers. "Not bad."

"Looks good on you. Ready?"

Alexei ordered a car from his cell phone, and a driver picked them up in front of the hotel.

Britt didn't know the name of the street where she'd left her car, so she gave the driver the address of Rage.

The driver adjusted his rearview mirror. "A guy was killed over there last night."

Alexei squeezed her thigh. "We know. Terrible."

"Took the guy's wallet." The driver shook his head. "So not worth it, man. If someone wants my wallet, they can have it."

When they reached Sunset, Britt hunched forward in the back seat. "I think it's…that street. You can just drop us at the corner."

He let them out, and Britt started walking down the block, her heart pounding. "I don't see my car."

"Are you sure this is the street? Maybe it was the next one over."

"I know it's this street because of the signal at the intersection. The two blocks on either side of this one don't have a signal at Sunset."

Alexei cleared his throat and grabbed a pole with a street sign on it. "This street is permit parking only."

"Yeah, I know that. I didn't think I'd be leaving my car overnight. Where the hell is it, then?"

"You'll have to call the LA sheriff's department. They'll tell you where your car is, and you can pick it up." Crossing his arms, Alexei wedged his shoulder against the pole. "I'll get you another car to take you to the tow yard, and I'll get myself back to the hotel. Do you need money to get it out?"

"No." She kicked the pole. "I completely forgot I was parked illegally. You can't come with me?"

"Don't think it's a great idea for us to be seen together."

"I feel like I'm the other woman." She should be so lucky.

He tugged on a strand of her hair. "I'll wait with you while you call the police, and I'll call another car."

Fifteen minutes later as the share car pulled up to the curb, Britt clutched her cell phone, where she'd entered the name and address of the tow yard she'd gotten from the sheriff's department.

Alexei opened the back door of the car for her, and she placed her hand on his arm. "Will you be at the club tonight?"

"Yeah. I talked to a few guys last night, and I want to continue my progress with them. Besides, I don't want to leave you on your own there."

She curled her fingers into his flesh. "First Leanna, now Jerome. I'm not going to let them get away with this. Someone is going to have to pay."

She expected him to shrug off her fierce

declaration, but he wedged his knuckle beneath her chin and tilted back her head, his dark blue eyes smoldering.

"Someone *is* going to pay if I have anything to say about it."

As she watched him from the back window of the car, she had the distinct feeling that Alexei had his own agenda.

STANDING BEFORE THE mirror in the dressing room for the dancers, Britt flattened her hands against her new black skirt and smoothed it against her thighs. Her gaze flicked away from her own reflection to the scene behind her—some of the dancers sniffling about Jerome's death, others hugging each other, and some of the women over it already and slipping into their barely there costumes.

Sergei had given a rousing give-'em-hell speech after announcing the murder of Jerome, telling the waitresses and dancers to get out on the floor and do their best because that was what Jerome would've wanted. Britt curled her lip at her image. She sincerely doubted that.

She turned away from the mirror, hands on her hips, and surveyed the chaotic scene before her. Still no sign of Jessie. Had she heard about the murder earlier and called in sick?

Or had something happened at the rehearsal last night?

Britt's stomach rolled. When she took this job, she figured she'd poke around, maybe overhear a few choice conversations and collect enough evidence to either find Leanna or go to the police. She never imagined she'd land right in the middle of a human-trafficking ring with a Russian crime family working with terrorists.

She never imagined she'd meet a man like Alexei Ivanov either.

She tucked her purse between two others on the bench next to the dressing room door. Another waitress squeezed in beside her and wedged her bag among the line of purses.

Britt put her hand on the waitress's arm. "Amy, have you seen Jessie tonight?"

"She called in sick. Shannon is subbing for her shift."

"Because of Jerome?"

Shrugging her shoulders, Amy pushed out of the dressing room.

Britt followed Amy out to the bar, where Sergei had set up a tip jar with Jerome's picture taped to the rim. Nice of him to take up a collection for the family of the man he had murdered.

She grabbed a notepad from the stack next

to the collection jar and nodded at the new bartender. "Hi, I'm Barbie."

He studied her from beneath a pair of bushy eyebrows and hesitated so long she thought he hadn't heard her. Then he held out his hand. "Stepan. You dancer?"

"No."

He immediately released her hand.

"I'm a waitress. Are you new, Stepan, or from one of the other clubs?"

His curious brows turned into suspicious ones as they created a V over his nose. "I work here and there. Wherever they need me."

Ah, a loyal Belkin follower. Stepan wouldn't be sneaking back into the club after hours or crying on a missing waitress's bed. Sergei had learned his lesson.

Alexei still hadn't been able to tell her why the Belkins had killed Jerome. They couldn't have known that he was in the club that night, because Alexei had cleaned that video. Had Jerome been up to other suspicious activity? Had they known about his connection with Leanna?

A chill raced down her arms. If having a connection to Leanna could get you murdered, what would Sergei do to Leanna's sister?

The doors had opened, and patrons began filling the tables that bordered the stage.

Britt's heart jumped every time she caught sight of a tall man with dark hair, but Alexei hadn't appeared with the first wave of customers.

At the bar on a drink run, Britt stationed herself next to Shannon, the waitress filling in for Jessie. "Did you talk to Jessie? Is she sick?"

"I didn't talk to her." Shannon rapped her knuckles on the mahogany of the bar. "Hey, Stepan. This margarita is supposed to be blended, not on the rocks. Redo."

Without a word, Stepan snatched the drink from the tray.

Shannon rolled her eyes. "He's no Jerome, is he?"

"That was so terrible. I still can't believe he was killed in that awful way." Britt busied herself by arranging the drinks on her tray. "D-do you think that's why Jessie took the night off?"

"I didn't think they were that close. Jerome kind of kept to himself."

Snapping fingers appeared between their faces, and Britt jerked back, almost stumbling against Sergei right behind her.

"No talking about Jerome. Didn't you hear me? We take up collection, but this is happy place for happy people."

"We weren't talking in front of the customers. Chill." Shannon hoisted her tray of drinks and pushed past Sergei.

Sergei glanced at Stepan, pointed to his own eye and then made his fingers into a gun, pointing it at Shannon's back.

When he caught Britt looking at him, Sergei raised one shoulder. "She's a pain, that one. Don't ever be a pain, Barbie Doll."

"Hey, I'm just here to do my job." She grabbed her own drink tray. "By the way, how did Jessie do at her audition last night?"

Sergei splayed his fingers in the air and tipped his hand back and forth. "My socks still on."

Britt allowed herself a tight smile before escaping from his presence. Maybe Sergei told Jessie she wasn't good enough to be a dancer and Jessie left in a snit.

When Britt dropped her first order, she glanced toward the door and locked eyes with Alexei. She let out a breath. He was still alone. Was he hoping to make more contacts tonight? Did those contacts include Sergei?

Of course, Alexei didn't take a seat in her section. It made it that much harder to talk to him casually. Maybe he wanted her to stay away.

She needed to tell him about Sergei's response to Jerome's murder and that Jessie hadn't shown up for work, but maybe he didn't want to hear about all that. He hadn't come out here to investigate the Belkins' sex-trafficking operation. Her drama must be keeping him from his true purpose. Maybe Alexei was right and she should just go back to Charlotte.

If in the course of doing his job Alexei found Leanna, he'd tell her. He might even go out of his way a little to discover Leanna's whereabouts. She needed to let him do his job.

Alexei had sat at a table close enough to her own station that she had an excuse to make contact. Squeezing past his table, she knocked over his drink.

"I'm so sorry." She crouched next to the table, mopping the spill with some cocktail napkins. "Did you see the tip jar for Jerome on the bar?"

"No. That's big of him."

"Sergei doesn't want us talking about Jerome in this happiest of places on earth."

"I'll bet he doesn't. Anything else unusual tonight?"

"Jessie, one of the waitresses, auditioned for a place on the stage last night and she didn't come into work today."

"Was she close to Jerome?"

"I don't think so." She dropped a wad of

soggy napkins on her tray. "One of the other women said Jerome hadn't been close to anyone...except Leanna, although nobody seemed aware of their relationship. How do you think Sergei knew about it?"

"We don't know if that's why he offed Jerome. It could be something else, like why Jerome was sneaking around here after hours. I cleaned one tape, but what if there were others and Sergei got an eyeful of Jerome on one of his nighttime visits to the club? We don't know what Jerome was doing here."

"I'd better get moving or the others are going to wonder why I'm polishing this table."

"I don't want you leaving here alone tonight. Tell me where you're parked, and I'll follow you home on my bike."

"I'm in the alley, but two businesses down from this one."

"Any trouble getting your car today?"

"Nope. I paid the tow yard, and they released my car."

"Okay. Be careful tonight, but I'm right here if you need me."

Britt finished the remainder of her shift with her heart in a warm bubble. She owed it to Alexei to get out of his way. He'd become preoccupied with protecting her, and although she had no complaints, he had his own job to do. He'd joined a couple of other men at their table, so she hoped he was making headway in his own investigation.

At the end of the night without even looking at Alexei's table, she knew he'd left. The room almost felt colder, her protective shell a flimsy thing.

Sergei and Irina had called it quits almost an hour ago and Stepan was shouting orders and ogling the dancers at the same time.

To escape the tyrant, Britt joined the dancers as they streamed into the changing room. She deserved to duck out early. What could they do, fire her? She would quit before that happened.

The purses crammed on the bench inside the dressing room must've reached critical mass, as several of them had fallen onto the floor, including hers.

Britt dropped to her knees and started shoveling items back into her purse—wallet, phone. Her breath hitched when she realized anyone could've gone through her things, but she kept her driver's license under the seat in her car, and she'd password-protected her phone, even though Alexei had been worried about the pictures on it.

Opening her purse wide, she bounced it a few times to redistribute the items. She bit her bottom lip, plunged her hand into her purse and rooted to the bottom of it. The receipt from the tow yard must've fallen out.

She tilted her head sideways and peered under the bench. She pinched one receipt between her fingertips, but it was too small to be the tow receipt, and it belonged to someone else.

She sat back on her heels, scanning the floor for the receipt. Then it hit her.

The receipt indicated the address where her car was parked when it had been towed. If the wrong person saw that, he'd know she'd been in the area where Jerome had been murdered.

She flattened her body against the carpeted floor for a better look under the bench.

"What are you doing down there?"

Britt twisted her head to the side, meeting one of the dancers' heavily lined eyes. "My purse fell off the bench, and I'm missing something."

"Money?"

"A receipt."

She shrugged and waved her fingers at the bags shoved against each other helter-skelter. "Maybe in someone else's purse. You should look."

Britt didn't want to bring any more attention to the receipt than she already had with the dancer, Gypsy, so she poked around in a few purses but didn't see her receipt in any of them.

"Find it?" Gypsy hitched her own purse over her shoulder.

"No. Maybe someone threw it away."

"Was it important?"

"Not really."

Gypsy swept out of the room and knocked the purse on the end of the bench to the floor. Britt sighed. Management needed to find a better place for purses, or maybe they did it on purpose to search their employees' bags.

She gathered the spilled contents of the purse and started shoveling the items back inside. A drawing on the back of a business card caught her eye, and she dragged it close with her finger for a better look.

She caught her breath and shot a quick glance over her shoulder at the two dancers talking in front of the mirror. She traced her finger over the snake wrapped around the letter *B*—the tattoo Tatyana had on her forearm—the sign of the Belkins.

She flipped the card over. The name and address of a tattoo parlor in Hollywood occupied the other side. Britt slipped the card in the pocket of her skirt.

If someone had taken her receipt, she could play the same game.

She placed the purse back on the bench. She'd find something else to do in the changing room and wait for the owner. She pulled out her phone and pretended to scroll through texts, but she didn't have to wait long.

One of the women chatting by the mirror pulled her blouse over her head. "I see you tomorrow night, Tracy."

She snagged the purse on the end and exited the dressing room with a wave to Britt.

Britt tucked her phone back into her purse. "Pretty girl. What's her name, Tracy? I still don't have everyone's name down."

"That's Mila. She's from some little village in the Ukraine. They come out here with stars in their eyes, hoping to make it in Hollywood, and they wind up in joints like this." Tracy dragged a tissue across her mouth to wipe off the bright red lipstick. "Or worse."

"Worse?"

Tracy put a finger to her pale pink lips. "How about you? Do you have aspirations to be a dancer, or are you happy slinging drinks?"

"I'm a waitress, and that's okay with me. I just stumbled on this place because the club was hiring, and Irina told me there was an opportunity to make a little extra money working parties for Sergei's family."

"The Tattle-Tale always has openings—high turnover. I'm leaving myself pretty soon."

"Why?"

"Moving to Vegas with my boyfriend. He's a dealer, and as soon as he gets a job at one of the casinos out there, I'm gone."

"Seems to be an epidemic of that."

"What?" Tracy brushed past Britt to claim her own purse.

Britt lowered her voice. "Women leaving the Tattle-Tale to take off with their boyfriends. Jessie told me another waitress left to go off with her boyfriend."

Tracy dipped her head and dug through her bag, pulling out her keychain. She swung it around her finger. "I didn't hear that. Gotta go."

Britt looked around the empty dressing room. How many people suspected something was off at the Tattle-Tale? Tracy seemed anxious to be on her way once she'd mentioned the other waitress leaving with her boyfriend. Or had she imagined that?

Another bunch of women bustled into the room, chattering. Stepan must've corralled them into cleaning up, and Britt didn't want to be caught by Stepan.

She exchanged a few words with some of the women, who were complaining about Stepan, and then slipped into the hallway and out the back door. She'd kept Alexei waiting long enough.

"Hello, Barbie."

Britt jumped, hugging her purse to her chest. She let out a breath when she saw Calvin pushing his cart. "How are you doing, Calvin?"

"Brilliant."

"You need a few bucks?"

Calvin muttered to himself and shuffled past her.

Britt dug a couple of bills out of her tip money and tucked them into the pocket of Calvin's tattered jacket as she walked by. "Just in case."

She strode to her car, holding the remote in front of her to unlock it. Several of the bars on this stretch of the boulevard had back doors, and most of the parking in the alley was reserved for the employees of these businesses, so Britt had more company than just Calvin. And Alexei had to be watching from somewhere on his bike.

When she slipped onto the front seat and

started her engine, she detected a single head-light at a distance behind her. She wanted to let him know about her missing receipt and about the tattoo-parlor card, but he hadn't given her his cell number. Hadn't wanted his number on her phone, but they had to have a better way of contacting each other than fe-vered conversations at the Tattle-Tale.

She turned out of the alley onto the street and joined the light traffic. Although there were quite a few bars in this area, all closing at 2:00 a.m., this stretch of road in Hollywood didn't compare to the glut of clubs and bars on that piece of real estate on the Sunset Strip where Jerome had been murdered. Still, she felt safe with Alexei on her tail.

She figured he knew her address, but she signaled at every turn anyway until she turned onto her street lined with apartment buildings.

She parked at the curb a few buildings down from her own. At least she had the right per-mit to park on this street.

To her surprise, Alexei pulled up on his bike behind her.

As she got out of the car, he cut his engine. Putting her hand on her hip, she said, "Aren't you afraid to be seen here?"

He lifted the helmet from his head. "There's

nobody around. Nobody followed you. Everything okay?"

"Not exactly."

"What happened?"

"I—I lost the receipt for my car."

He swung his leg over his bike. "The tow yard?"

"Yeah, the receipt that shows where I was parked last night—right in the vicinity where Jerome was attacked."

"You lost it at the club?" He ran a hand through his hair, making it stand up on end even more than the helmet did.

"I don't know if *lost* is the right word. The purses in the dressing room had fallen over. I noticed the receipt was gone when I was putting my stuff back in my bag."

He kicked the toe of his boot against the curb. "That's not good. What about your name? Is your real name on the receipt?"

"I am Barbie Jones here in LA. I have a driver's license, car registration and apartment lease to prove that. The receipt is for Barbie Jones."

His eyebrows shot up. "How'd you manage that?"

"Don't ask."

"Okay, so the name on the receipt will check out, but the address where your car was parked is a problem—if someone didn't just throw it away or one of the other women accidentally put it in her purse."

"I hope that's the case, but there's more."

"That new bartender?"

"A piece of work, but it's not him." She drew the card from her pocket and handed it to Alexei.

He held it up to the streetlight a few feet away. "What is it? It's too dark out here—no moon."

"It's a business card for a tattoo parlor." She took her phone from her purse and flicked on the flashlight, holding it over the card pinched between his fingers. "Turn it over."

He whistled. "Who had this?"

"One of the dancers—a girl named Mila."

"Russian?"

"Ukrainian."

"I wonder if they're sending her in for a tattoo."

"We need to stop her. She can't know that's the next step to joining their sex ring."

"Maybe she does, maybe she doesn't. I'm keeping this." The card disappeared into the pocket of his jacket. "I'm going to walk you up. This isn't a great area."

"It's the best I could do." She crooked her finger. "This way."

She led Alexei up to the second floor via a set of stairs on the outside of the '50s-style apartment building, a coat of stucco slapped on its sides, not too different from Leanna's place, except these individual apartments created a horseshoe around a sad little courtyard with some droopy palm trees stationed in the four corners.

Britt slid her key home in the dead bolt and then twisted it in the door-handle lock. She'd left a lamp on in the furnished living room, just like she always did.

When she stepped over the threshold, she tripped to a stop and covered her mouth. The lamp was the only thing the same as she'd left it.

Chapter Seven

Alexei widened his eyes. Britt Jansen was either a slob or someone had tossed her place, and by the way her shoulders were stiffening, Britt was no slob.

He pulled his gun out of his pocket and touched her back with his other hand. She jumped.

"Sorry." Grabbing her sleeve, he dragged her back, behind him. "How many rooms?"

"It's an old-style bachelor. This room and a bathroom over there." She pointed an unsteady finger at a door to the right.

"I'm assuming you didn't leave your place like this."

Her gaze darted to the weapon in his hand as she shook her head.

"Stay here while I check out the bathroom. When I tell you it's clear, close and lock the front door."

"And if it's not clear?" She eyed the bathroom door.

"Run like hell."

He crept toward the bathroom, although if the intruder were hiding in the shower, he would've heard them by now. No need for stealth—just firepower. Leading with his gun, Alexei kicked open the bathroom door. It shuddered and swung open on an empty room.

He yelled over his shoulder. "Clear. Lock that door."

The front door slammed, and seconds later Britt joined him at the entrance to the bathroom, hovering over his shoulder, pinching his sleeve. "They know."

"Check to see if anything's missing." His pulse jumped and he jerked, banging his shoulder with hers. "The painting of Tatyana."

The color drained from her face. "I hid it."

"Where?"

She took his hand, pulling him out of the bathroom behind her. "When I moved in, the landlady pointed out some loose floorboards by the window. Of course, she hasn't fixed them yet and probably won't."

She dropped to her knees in front of the window that looked out on the courtyard. She flicked back a worn area rug, and using her key, she jimmied the edge of one of the slats of wood.

"Hang on." He slid a knife from his pocket and flicked the blade. He inserted it along the crack between two of the floorboards and jiggled it. He pried up one of the boards and flipped it up, exposing a dark cavity beneath the floor. "Can you tell if it's there without pulling up the whole floor?"

She lay on her belly and aimed her phone into the space. "I see it. It's still there."

She rolled over onto her back, flinging one arm across her face. "Thank God they didn't find it, but they suspect me. It must be the tow-yard receipt. Do you think that's it?"

"Unless Sergei makes a habit out of searching new waitress's apartments, he must've had his goons come here for a reason."

He rose from his crouch and extended his hand to her. "It's a good thing you had the brilliant idea to hide the painting. If the intruder had seen that, there would've been no suspicion left in Sergei's mind that you were going to pose a problem."

She grasped his hand, and he pulled her to her feet.

Brushing off the front of her clothes, she asked, "And the tow-yard receipt? What does that tell him?"

"Tells him you were in the area when Jerome was murdered. Lots of people go to that part of town at that time of night. The killer didn't see Jerome with you or anyone else."

"I have an idea." She slumped into one of the two chairs in the room. "I can confess to a couple of the girls that I was supposed to meet Jerome for a drink that night, had trouble parking, and by the time I got to Rage, Jerome had been killed. I was too afraid to talk to the cops."

Alexei took the other chair and hunched forward, his elbows digging into his knees. "Why do you need a story when you're leaving?"

Britt's chin formed a hard line that he was beginning to recognize.

"Who said I was leaving? Mila is at risk. Jessie is missing. We can't let the Belkins continue to use young women and destroy them and their dreams."

He clasped his hands and rested his chin on his interlocked knuckles. Britt not only wanted to save her sister, but she also wanted to rescue every woman in that club.

"Britt, what I'm working on will bring down the Belkins and all of their operations in LA, including their sex-trafficking ring. I made some contacts, and I'm hoping to get invited to one of their parties at the banquet hall."

"What if it's too late for Mila?"

"It's not your job to save Mila, not if it compromises your own safety." He pushed out of the chair and wandered to the window. "Are you trying to compensate for not being here to save your sister?"

As soon as the words left his mouth, before he even heard Britt's breath hiss between her teeth, he knew he'd made another boorish blunder.

The chair squeaked behind him, and she joined him at the window, her face tight. "Are you trying to psychoanalyze me?"

He turned toward her and rubbed his hands up and down her stiff arms. "I'm sorry. It's none of my business why you want to help Mila, and I'm not implying that the only reason is that you see her as some kind of substitute for Leanna."

She lifted her shoulders. "That's okay. As a therapist, I'm self-aware enough to know my motivations. Doesn't make them any less compelling."

"I just don't want to see you put yourself in danger anymore, although I guess that's not any of my business either."

Her eyelashes fluttered, and his pulse quickened. Did she want her safety to be his business?

He swept his arm behind him, encompassing the room. "We know whoever broke in didn't get the painting of Tatyana, but what did he get? You haven't checked to see if anything else was missing. Laptop?"

"My laptop's in the car." She drove the heel of her hand against her forehead. "I left it there, under the seat."

"We'll get it in a minute. It's a good thing you had it there. Do you make a habit of taking it with you to the club?"

"I don't have Wi-Fi here. I stopped at a coffeehouse on the way to the Tattle-Tale tonight so I could check emails and catch up on a little work. I do still have clients who need me."

Who didn't need Britt?

"Anything else?" He spread his arms. "No notes from Leanna or pictures tying her to you? Those bills?"

"Look at this place." She ducked around him and opened and closed the door of the microwave, which was the extent of her kitchen in here. "Bare bones, and I paid her bills and tossed them."

"So, all they have on you is a receipt from a tow yard, indicating you were in the vicinity when they murdered Jerome—unless they don't have the receipt at all and you've given them some other reason to suspect you."

"There's nothing, and I'm going to alleviate Sergei's suspicions about the tow-yard receipt."

"By spreading it around that you were in the area that night?"

"I'm going to admit that I was supposed to meet Jerome—for a date."

"Is that a good idea considering they'd pegged Jerome as public enemy number one? They must've had something on him to eliminate him like that."

"He knew something about Tatyana or about Leanna's disappearance."

"Or both."

"Doesn't mean he told me."

He dropped into a chair and drummed his finger against the arm of it. "I wonder what Jerome was doing at the Tattle-Tale that night he returned when we were there and if it had anything to do with his murder."

"But Sergei never saw him come back because you did that voodoo on the tape and erased Jerome's late-night visit."

"Maybe that wasn't Jerome's first late-night visit back to the club. Maybe he'd done that before and Sergei *did* see him on the surveillance video."

"Did you even pay attention to what he was doing when he came back? I didn't. I was too freaked out."

"He went behind the bar, but I don't recall what part of it or what he did back there, but—" he snapped his fingers "—we can replay it. I have that video on my laptop."

"That might help. I have a better idea now what's what behind the bar and may be able to make some educated guesses about what Jerome was doing there, but that means I am going back to the Tattle-Tale, and I'm going to drop the word about me and Jerome. Sergei can believe what he wants." Britt wedged her hands on her hips as if expecting to do battle.

"All right, but you're not going to be there on your own. I met a guy tonight, another Russian, and he's going to introduce me to Sergei tomorrow night, or I guess I met him last night, and he's introducing me to Sergei tonight."

"You're not introducing yourself as Alexei Ivanov, are you?"

Alexei's lips curled into a smile. As much as he'd like to see the look on Sergei's face when he heard the name Alexei Ivanov, he wasn't ready for that yet. "I'm Mikhail Orloff—Mickey."

Britt winked. "Barbie and Mickey—I like it."

He liked it, too, liked her and everything about her.

"Better than Barbie and Ken." He jerked a thumb over his shoulder. "Get your things, and let's go, Barbie."

She wrinkled her nose. "Go where?"

"My hotel in Beverly Hills. Do you think I'm going to let you stay in this dump after it's already been compromised?"

"What happened to not being seen together?" Her cheeks flushed a pretty pink.

"Nobody connected to the Belkins or the Tattle-Tale is going to see us in Beverly Hills, especially not at that hotel. You can't stay here, Britt. It's not safe. It never was."

"All right. Give me a few minutes to pack my stuff." She walked to the window and kicked aside the carpet. "Why don't you get the painting?"

As he crouched down to lift the floorboards, she threw open a set of accordion closet doors.

"I take that back. My little jewelry case is missing."

He looked up from trying to squeeze his arm into the cavity. "Anything of value?"

"No, just some costume pieces. Maybe Sergei told whoever broke in to make it look like a random burglary." She turned, holding a dress to her chest. "Do you think it could've been?"

"Doubt it. It's just too coincidental. How would a random thief know you were out tonight? Why would he chance it? I'm sorry but why would a burglar even hit a bachelor like this? You don't even have a TV."

"Don't worry. You're not offending me." She hauled a suitcase from the closet onto the daybed, which must double as her bed.

He returned to the project of removing the painting, and Britt stopped shoveling clothes into her bag. "I don't think you're ever going to get your arm in there without removing the next floorboard. Hang on. I'll get it."

She knelt beside him, and the ends of her hair tickled his arm as she bent over the gap in the floor. "Let me."

Her slim arm disappeared into the floor, and she retrieved the rolled-up paper and dropped it. "I think I need to find a better place than this."

"There's a safe at the hotel. We'll stash it there." He tipped his head toward her bag. "Do you have everything you need?"

"In case they come back, I don't want it to look like I moved out, so I'll leave a few things."

Britt finished packing and locked up the apartment.

Before Alexei got on his bike, he said, "Pull

up to the valet parking attendant, and leave your car with him. Meet me at the room."

About thirty minutes later, Alexei sprang for the door after a soft knock. "What took you so long?"

Britt patted his arm as she breezed past him, wheeling her bag behind her. "He's gotta get to my car, give me my ticket, I gotta give him a tip. These things take time." She collapsed on the couch. "I'm exhausted."

"No kidding." He held up the painting. "I'm going to put this in the closet for now and see about getting it locked up tomorrow. You can have the bathroom first, and the bed's all yours."

"Mmm." She fell onto her side and curled up her legs.

When he went into the bedroom, he ran his hand along the freshly made bed and then turned down the covers. The maid had hung the shirt Britt had worn the night before on the back of a chair, and Alexei plucked it up and pressed it against his face. He inhaled Britt's scent from the folds of the cotton.

Was he crazy inviting her back here? What else could he do to keep her safe, other than send her home to North Carolina? Britt was no puppet to be jerked this way and that. She wanted to stay at the Tattle-Tale, and he wasn't just making excuses for himself. He couldn't order her about.

He dropped the T-shirt on the chair and ducked into the closet. He propped up the painting in the corner in the back.

When he returned to the sitting room of the suite, Britt's cheek rested on her hand, and her hair trailed off the edge of the sofa.

He nudged her shoulder once, and she murmured in her sleep.

If he carried her to the bed, she might wake up, and she looked so peaceful, the little crease of worry between her brows finally smoothed out. If he carried her to the bed, he might be tempted to crawl in beside her.

He shook out the blanket the maid had folded at the bottom of the sofa and tucked it around Britt. With one finger, he smoothed the hair from her face and whispered, "Good night, *moya solnishka.*"

BRITT ORDERED ANOTHER iced tea from the poolside waitress and stretched her arms over her head, reaching for the sun. She tipped her glasses on top of her head and squinted at a boisterous group at the other end of the pool deck. Was that a celebrity with his entourage?

Sighing, she curled her toes. She could get used to lounging at a rooftop pool overlooking the palm-lined streets of Beverly Hills. The only improvement would be having Alexei beside her, but he'd headed out this afternoon for some secret meetings in an effort to solidify his fake identity and get invited to the party at the Belkins' banquet hall.

When the waitress returned with her tea, Britt held it over her body, letting the cold drops from the sweating glass hit the warm skin of her belly. The sun had finally broken through the marine layer, and it was baking all the pretty people at the pool—not that her mission included fun in the sun, but after the few days she'd had since meeting Alexei, she needed some downtime.

Her immediate goal tonight included offering an excuse for being in the area when Jerome was murdered...and getting close to Mila to see if she'd gotten the tattoo yet.

"Don't get burned."

Shading her eyes, she glanced up at Alexei, towering over her. The crisp suit he wore fit him like a glove, and her mouth watered. She cleared her throat. "Sharp-dressed man."

"Playing the part." He sat down on the edge of the chaise lounge next to hers and hunched forward, the material of his jacket stretching across his muscled shoulders.

She blinked and adjusted her sunglasses. "Did you get your invitation to the party?"

"Almost have it nailed down. I'm meeting an FOS at the Tattle-Tale tonight."

"An FOS?"

"Friend of Sergei. Turns out Sergei has a lot of friends that I'm sure his father doesn't even know about. Makes my job of infiltrating the inner circle easier, but Sergei had better hope Olav never finds out how fast and loose he's been with his favors."

"Olav is Sergei's father?"

"Yes."

Alexei almost spit out the word, and it hung between them as Britt waited for the rest of the story on Belkin the elder. Several awkward seconds later, she realized she wasn't going to get it.

The chaise lounge creaked as Alexei rose. "Dinner in the room before you head out for your shift?"

She nodded. Through narrowed eyes she watched Alexei's back as he walked toward the elevator. He had something going on with the Belkin family he wasn't sharing with her. It probably wasn't any of her business, but she wished he'd trust her enough to tell her the whole truth behind his mission.

Of course, once that mission came to its

successful conclusion, she'd never see Alexei Ivanov again. She closed her eyes and pressed the cold glass against her cheek.

And she wasn't ready for that.

LATER THAT NIGHT, Britt scanned the Tattle-Tale as she grabbed a pad of paper from the top of the bar. She tapped Stepan on the arm with a pen. "Do you know if Jessie is working tonight?"

He lifted and dropped one shoulder. "Jessie, Jessie, I don't know Jessie. All girls the same here."

She rolled her eyes. "Yeah, you mean none of them will go out with you."

Stepan's hand shot out, and he grabbed her wrist, cinching his fingers around it. "Not like the other guy, eh? I hear you supposed to go out with other guy. Didn't work out."

She jerked her arm away from his grasp. "At least Jerome had some class."

"Had."

Britt spun away from Stepan with her heart pounding. So her story had gotten around already. She'd told a couple of the other waitresses about her ill-fated date with Jerome. Hopefully that would answer any lingering suspicions Sergei had about her presence on Sunset the night he'd had Jerome murdered.

A tap on her shoulder had Britt clenching her fist and jerking around.

Irina's penciled-in brows shot up. "Are you okay, Barbie?"

"Sorry." Britt blew out a sigh. "I thought you were Stepan."

"That man—" Irina slid a sideways glance at the bar "—doesn't belong here. We will get someone new soon. Let me know if he is bothering you. Can you come to the office with me for a minute?"

"Of course." Britt pressed a hand against her belly, where nervous knots twisted. Had they found out she was Lee's sister? Was she going to be fired for dating Jerome? Had they noticed her talking to Alexei?

Irina led her to Sergei's office, where Britt had last been with Alexei, and waved her into the chair across from Sergei's desk.

"I hear from a few other girls that you were going to meet Jerome the night he was killed."

"Yes, that's right." Britt twisted her fingers in her lap. "I'm sorry if that's not allowed. That's why I didn't tell anyone and then when…" She covered her eyes with one hand.

"It's not against rules, but we don't encourage it. Jerome should've known better." Irina reached up and twirled one of the studs in her ear. "Did you see anything that night? Should you talk to police? I don't think they've found the man who killed Jerome."

Britt's head shot up, and she widened her eyes. "I don't want to talk to the police. I didn't see anything. I was late, so I parked illegally. When I came around the corner of Sunset, the police were already there, and when I saw it was Jerome lying on the sidewalk, I ran away. I ducked into a bar down the street, and I... got drunk. I'm ashamed to say it, but I was freaked out. I-it was a robbery, right? That's what I heard."

"It was robbery. His wallet and watch were stolen."

"I hope this isn't going to get me fired. I really need this job right now. On top of everything, my car was towed that night, and I had to pay to get it out of the tow yard, and to add insult to injury, someone broke into my apartment last night and stole my jewelry." She ended the last syllable on a whine for maximum effect.

The door swung open, and Sergei stepped inside the small office, immediately overwhelming it with the scent of his cologne.

Had he been listening at the door? She hoped so.

"Nobody getting fired, Barbie Doll. You need extra cash? We need one more waitress."

"I'm already working tonight." Britt half rose from her chair. "In fact, I'd better get out there now since the club already opened."

"I'm talking about another gig. We throw big party tomorrow night. One of the waitresses not going, so you take her place." He reached over and patted her cheek. "Just no more dating bartenders, eh?"

Britt licked her lips. She'd be at the same party as Alexei, at the banquet hall. She might even get an opportunity to meet Olav Belkin, the head of the crime family.

"Thank you. Yes, I'd like to work." She scooted past Sergei and paused at the office door. "Which of the waitresses backed out of the party?"

"Jessie." Sergei snapped his fingers in dismissal. "Worthless girl. Quit when she didn't get dancing job."

Britt nodded and gritted her back teeth through her smile as she backed out of the office. What had happened to Jessie?

The next hour, she worked her tables in a fog. Nobody seemed to know anything about Jessie, and Britt was afraid to show too much interest in the other waitress's whereabouts.

When she spotted Alexei seated at a table with two other men, she snapped out of her fog. She had no way to communicate with him tonight, but then she'd be seeing him back at the hotel after her shift.

He'd warned her to make absolutely sure nobody followed her from the club. He'd be keeping a safe distance on his bike to run interference in case he noticed something.

Alexei and his party had a table of honor, front and center, courtesy of Sergei—and as the newest waitress, she didn't rate those tables.

At the end of the night, Britt made a point of crowding into the changing room with the dancers so she could talk to Mila, who was primping at the mirror.

Britt spied a tube of lipstick on the floor and kicked it toward the mirror. She followed the silver cylinder and bent forward, sweeping it up in one movement. "Did you drop this?"

Mila turned from the mirror, her hand still raised in mid-mascara stroke. "No, that is not mine. Vera?"

"Not mine."

Britt dropped her gaze to Mila's slender arms, unblemished by any tattoos, and let out a long breath. The dancer hadn't made it to the tattoo parlor yet. And when she did?

Britt's gaze darted around the room at the other dancers. None of them sported tattoos—

at least not the *B* with the snake on the underside of their forearms.

What happened to the women once they got the tattoo? Was dancing in one of the Belkins' clubs the first step to working in their stable?

Had Leanna discovered all of this? Surely, more than a few of the women must have some clue about that side of the Belkins' operation. It didn't have to be a death sentence.

Then why get rid of Tatyana? Leanna? Jerome? Was she next? Britt shivered. She wouldn't be next with Alexei on her side.

She grabbed her purse from the bench. "Night, all."

She slipped out the back door of the club and hitched her bag over her shoulder as she trudged to her car. None of the shadows or noises in the alley scared her because she knew Alexei was close by.

A rattling sound came barreling up behind her, and she jumped to the side. Calvin rolled past her, his feet on the edge of his shopping cart.

"You in a hurry, Calvin?"

"No, just enjoying summer. No overcast skies today."

"It was beautiful." Britt dug into her pocket and pulled out a handful of her tip money. She called after Calvin. "I got something for you."

Calvin dragged his foot on the ground to slow down his basket and made a U-turn. He pushed his gray hair out of his eyes before holding out his hand.

Britt crumpled the bills into his palm, and he closed his hand around her fingers, his grip stronger than she'd expected. When she tried to pull away, he tightened his hold, leaning in close, the alcohol on his breath fierce against her face.

His faded eyes glittered, and he whispered, "You're like her, like Lee-Low."

Chapter Eight

Britt sucked in a breath and grabbed the grimy sleeve of his shirt. "What do you know about Lee-Low?"

"Barbie? You okay?" Irina charged toward them down the alley. "Go away, you filthy man."

Calvin yanked away from Britt and skated away on his basket.

"You all right, Barbie?" Irina circled her finger at her temple. "He is crazy person."

"I'm okay. I was just giving him a little money, and he got excited."

Irina wrinkled her nose. "Don't encourage him. He hangs around here all the time. I call police once."

"He's harmless."

"I walk you to car anyway."

"Then who's going to walk you to your car?"

Irina winked and opened her purse wide

enough for Britt to see the gun tucked inside. "As Americans say, Misters Smith and Wesson walk me to car."

Swallowing, Britt gave Irina a weak smile.

Once she was safely in the driver's seat with the engine running and she saw Irina getting into her own car, Britt hugged the steering column and rested her forehead on top of the steering wheel.

What had just happened? How did Calvin know Leanna and what made him say she was like her?

Britt grabbed the edge of the rearview mirror and searched behind her for Calvin, but Irina had scared him off. Had Irina been trying to send her a message by showing her that weapon?

She rolled the car forward with her eyes still glued to the mirror. No single headlight lit up in the distance. Maybe Alexei had gotten tired of waiting for her. She pulled onto the boulevard, and like magic the solitary light appeared in the distance behind her like a comforting beacon. She made a few turns like Alexei had instructed her to do earlier, all the while watching her mirrors for any suspicious cars making the same turns. The only one following her was Alexei on his motorcycle.

It made her feel safe, although she'd had nothing but trouble in her life since the moment she ran into Alexei in Sergei's office. But if Alexei hadn't been there that night, Sergei would've seen her on the surveillance video and she might be dead...like Jerome. Like Jessie? Like Tatyana? Like...? No, she wouldn't go there. She had to talk to Calvin to find out what he knew about Leanna.

The manicured streets of Beverly Hills began to replace the grittier streets of Hollywood, and Britt breathed a little easier. Nobody but Alexei had followed her.

She dumped her car with the valet and nodded at the doorman as he jumped to open the door for her. She beat Alexei to the room and was waiting for him by the window when he walked in.

"Success." He pumped his fist in the air. "I got an invitation to the Belkins' party tomorrow night."

"So did I."

His eyebrows shot up to his messy hair. "You?"

"Sergei asked me to work."

"No!"

It was her turn to raise her eyebrows. "Excuse me?"

"Not a good idea." He shrugged off his jacket. "Do you know what goes on at those parties?"

"I'm thinking the exchange of a lot of information. Maybe I can even get a better look into the Belkin family organization."

"That's the Belkin family *crime* organization. How do you think those women with the tattoos get started?" He smacked a fist into his palm. "Parties like these."

"That's even better. If Leanna knew something about the sex trafficking, maybe I can find out what happened to her there."

"Doubt it." He raised a finger as if to shake it in her face and then thought better of it, collapsing in a chair and stretching his legs in front of him. "I suppose it's not going to do me any good to tell you not to go."

"Nope." She walked toward him and stepped over his long legs in her path. "I've got more to tell you."

"You always do. Were you able to convince everyone you had a date with Jerome the night he was killed?"

"I think so, but there's more." She sat on the edge of the sofa, crossing one leg over the other and kicking it back and forth to release her nervous energy. "Have you seen the homeless guy who hangs out in the alley behind the club?"

"I think so. Older guy with a basket?"

"Yeah—Calvin. I've talked to him a few times, given him some money, and tonight he told me I was like Lee-Low."

"He knew your sister?"

"Yeah. I was going to start grilling him, but Irina saw us and yelled at him, scared him off."

"She'd scare anyone off. Did she hear what you two were talking about?"

"She was too far away to hear anything, and then she showed me her gun in her purse."

"Doesn't surprise me."

"That she has a gun or that she showed it to me?"

"That she has one. She's at that club, working late—not the most upstanding clientele in that place."

"There was something else." Britt stopped kicking her leg and tucked her hands beneath her thighs. "The reason I'm working the gig tomorrow night is because Jessie canceled."

"Jessie?"

"I told you about her. She's a waitress, and she stayed late at the club the night that Jerome was murdered, and I haven't seen her since. She called in sick the next night, wasn't there tonight, and Sergei asked me to fill in for her at the party."

"Another disappearing woman." He held up three fingers and ticked them off. "Tatyana, Lee and now Jessie. I don't want there to be a fourth."

"There's not going to be a fourth."

"She says with confidence." He rose from the chair and joined her on the sofa. "How can you be so sure?"

Turning toward him, she cupped his stubbled jaw. "Because I have you."

Alexei's blue eyes darkened and kindled, as if a flame burned in their depths. He took her hand gently and turned it over, drilling a finger in the center of her palm. "You do have me...for now."

Britt snatched her hand away and jumped up from the couch. Did he have to be so brutally honest? Was she asking for forever?

Although she wouldn't mind forever. She pressed a hand to her warm cheek. He'd seen it in her face.

She had a careful mask that she wore in sessions with her clients, but she dropped it as soon as she left her office. If her clients could see her real face, the emotions playing across it as they unveiled their anxieties and fears and scary thoughts, they'd fire her. She made up for that stoicism on her off time—with a vengeance.

Alexei appeared next to her, resting one hand on her hip. "I mean, I'm here for as long as you need me."

She cracked a smile. "Be careful making promises you can't keep, Russki."

His hand slid to her waist, and the kiss he pressed against her lips tasted of vodka and expensive cigars and an aching truth.

She didn't mind truth. She accepted his kiss, on his terms…for now. It was all she had.

He whispered against her mouth, "I can't promise you anything more than tonight."

After she untangled her tongue from his, she whispered back, "I'm good with tonight."

He'd lifted her in his arms before she even knew what he was doing. When he carried her into the opulent suite's bedroom, she clung to him tighter, wanting to commit every detail to memory for future daydreams.

He poured her boneless form from his arms to the bed and pointed to his feet. "Need to get these motorcycle boots off first."

"Take your time." She toed off her sneakers and rubbed her tight calves. "I wouldn't mind trying out that shower in there with the two heads."

"Would be nice to scrub off the filth of that club from both of our bodies."

"I'll do yours if you do mine." She yanked her white blouse from the waistband of her skirt and unbuttoned the top two buttons. "There's even a towel-warming rack in there. I used it earlier."

"If you say so. I can't figure out half the things in that bathroom."

"I'll start warming up a couple of towels." She floated to the bathroom like she was walking on air, her feet barely touching the carpet.

She draped two fluffy towels over the warming rack and cranked on both showerheads. She shimmied out of her skirt and peeled off her blouse. She kicked both into the corner just as Alexei appeared at the door naked and so fine she didn't know where to look first.

She choked. "That was fast."

"Any complaints?"

"Does this look like complaining?" She pointed to the big smile on her face.

"And you—" he approached her like a panther assessing his prey "—are very, very slow."

He wrapped his arms around her and unhooked her bra. Then he slipped both of his hands into her underwear and cupped her bottom. Pulling her close, he speared her with his erection.

She sucked in a breath. "I thought we were going to shower first."

"We are, but I'm good at multitasking." And then he proved it by caressing her flesh and kissing her mouth, all while making her insides quake and quiver.

When he let her up for air, she held up her hand. "Hang on. I need to put my hair up."

While he tested the water spraying from the showerheads, Britt twisted her hair into a bun and shed her panties. She ran a hand down his back and muscled buttocks. "How's the water?"

"Perfect." Turning toward her, he encircled her waist with both hands. "Like everything else in here."

The cavernous shower had no door, no curtain, not even a border step into the wet tiles, and she and Alexei moved seamlessly into the warm jets.

The water hit the backs of his shoulders and trickled onto his chest, clinging to the black hair scattered there. She laid a hand between his pectoral muscles, spreading her fingers and curling them into his flesh. "My skin is so pale next to yours."

He cupped her breasts and then smoothed his hands down her sides and clamped them on her hips. "Your skin is so soft next to mine."

The huge shower suddenly seemed tiny and close, the spray beating down between her shoulder blades suddenly scorching hot. She leaned into him, her tongue darting along his collarbone, flicking at the droplets of water.

"You forgot washcloths, so I guess I'm going to have to use my hands to wash your body." He reached past her and cradled the bar of soap in his palm before lathering it between his hands.

"Oh well," she managed weakly.

He started just beneath her chin, his soapy hands skimming down her neck and shoulders, where he stopped to caress the knots that had been building there for days.

Circling his palms on her breasts, he said, "You have the most perfect breasts."

"Mmm." She closed her eyes as her nipples peaked and crinkled beneath his touch. "What makes a breast perfect?"

"The fact that they seem at home right here." He cradled her breasts with both hands, sluicing his thumbs across her nipples.

The electrifying sensation shot to her belly, and she grabbed his biceps. "You're turning me to jelly, and I need to do some exploring of my own before I'm too weak to lift one finger."

She soaped up her own hands and traced the muscles and hard edges of his body. She explored his body like a woman devoid of sight, her fingertips registering every dip and hard plane. The feel of him beneath her touch satisfied some deep urge within her that she couldn't name.

He shivered. "It feels like you're painting on my skin, making your mark."

She chewed on her lower lip. This was supposed to be a quickie hookup designed to slake their crazy thirst for each other, get it out of the way so that they could return to serious business without distraction.

She curled up one corner of her lip and ran her soapy hands along the length of his erection. "I'm just teasing you before the main event."

He growled and lunged forward. "Let's get to the main event on the bed. I don't want either one of us slipping in here and cracking our heads on this expensive tile."

They both stepped back under their showerheads and rinsed off, and the space between them gave Britt a shiver.

Alexei reached for the rack and yanked one towel free. "It worked. This is warm."

He pressed the towel against her, and she melted against the heated terry cloth. "That's nice. I'm going to have to consider one of those for my bathroom at home."

"Me, too." He grabbed the other towel.

He'd never even told her where home was.

Britt left the shower first, and the two small steps between her and Alexei yawned between them like a gulf. They'd shared a deep connection in that shower, one that she'd broken, one that Alexei had never wanted.

Her cell phone rang from the other room, and it acted like a prod, just like it had ever since the day her sister had gone missing.

"I have to get that." She tucked the towel around her body and scurried into the sitting room. The light from her phone glowed on the sofa where she'd left it.

She lunged for the cell and glanced at the unknown number as she answered. "Hello?"

A husky, harsh whisper replied. "The baby, find the baby."

Britt frowned at Alexei, who'd followed her out from the bedroom, wrapping his towel around his waist.

"I think you have the wrong number."

"You're Lee's sister."

Britt caught her breath. "Do you know where she is? Do you know where my sister is?"

A man's laughter from the background came over the line, and the caller's voice dropped even lower, her Russian accent more pronounced. "Find baby. Find baby and bring them all down."

"What baby? Whose baby?"

"Tatyana's baby."

Chapter Nine

Britt shouted into the phone. "Tatyana has a baby?"

Alexei's pulse jumped, and he mimicked pressing a button with his thumb to get Britt to put her phone on speaker.

"She's gone." Britt stared at the phone cupped in her trembling hand.

"Tatyana?" His gut churned. "Your sister?"

"No, no. The caller. She hung up."

"Who was she? What did she say? Tatyana has a baby?"

"I don't know who she was." Britt lifted her bare shoulders. "The caller had a Russian accent, and she knew I was Lee's sister. She said something about finding Tatyana's baby."

"What's that supposed to mean?" Alexei drilled two fingertips into his temple where a sharp pain lanced him. "How'd she get your number?"

"Leanna must've given it to her." She tipped the phone back and forth. "I can call her back."

"No!" The force of his exclamation startled Britt, causing her to drop the phone.

"Why not? She knows me, she knows Leanna and she knows Tatyana has a baby somewhere. I'd say she's a good place to start."

"You don't know who that was or whose phone she was using. What did she sound like, other than the Russian accent?"

"She was whispering. She sounded scared, nervous. I heard a man in the background."

"Exactly." Alexei bent forward and swept up the phone from the carpet. "Maybe she wasn't using her own phone. Do you really want to call back someone else's phone? Tip him off?"

"Whoever that is already has my number in his phone."

"If he notices the number and calls you back, you can play dumb. If it really is this woman's phone and she wants you to find Tatyana's baby, she'll call you back."

Britt crossed her arms, her balled fists digging into her sides. "What does it mean? She said find Tatyana's baby and bring them all down."

"Bring them down? If Tatyana was pregnant, she wouldn't be much use to the Belkins."

Alexei tapped the phone against his forehead. "Maybe that's why they got rid of her."

Britt's face blanched, and she plopped down on the edge of the sofa. "We couldn't figure out before why the Belkins would harm one of their women if she could turn a profit for them. Maybe that's what happened. Tatyana got pregnant, and the Belkins had no more use for her, but I still can't figure out where my sister fit in."

"Tatyana made the mistake of confiding in Leanna, and the Belkins found out."

She slumped against the sofa back. "Do you think there's a chance Leanna knew they were onto her and got away? When she sent me that text, she was worried about something. Leanna never worried about anything."

He knelt in front of her and tucked the towel more firmly around her body. "Let's keep that hope alive. Now, get some pajamas on and crawl between the sheets. It's late."

She jerked her head up, and the bun loosened, her blond hair falling around her shoulders like a cloud. "Y-you're joining me?"

"Britt." He took her hand and pressed a kiss in the middle of her palm. "That's probably not a good idea right now."

A smile trembled on her lips. "We've already sort of seen everything there is to see of each other. You can at least share the bed with me."

He folded her hand against his heart. "Believe me, it's a sight I won't soon forget, but if I'm lying next to you in that big bed, I don't think I could resist you."

She blinked at him.

"And I need to resist you."

She snatched her hand back and bounced up from the sofa. "Yeah, that's a good line. I'm sure you use it often. We'll discuss strategy tomorrow."

Brushing past him, she nearly toppled him over. She shut the bedroom door with a sharp click, which was way worse than a slam.

He fell face-first into the sofa and pounded his fists on the cushion. What the hell had he been thinking? If that phone call hadn't interrupted them, he'd be making love to Britt right now in that bedroom. That sounded great, better than great, at the moment, but what would happen when he left? When he got his next assignment? He didn't want anyone waiting for him.

His pregnant mother had waited for his father…and his father had never come home.

THE NEXT MORNING, Alexei woke up and pulled the tangled blanket to his chin, exposing his feet to the chilly air-conditioned room. He'd slept naked since he didn't dare go into the bedroom last night after Britt flounced out of here.

The bedroom door cracked open, and she stuck her head out. "Are you decent?"

He was about to remind her that she'd already seen his indecent side but thought better of it. Neither of them needed any reminders of last night.

He sat up on the sofa, pulling the blanket around his waist, eyeing her long legs extending from her shorts. "Yeah. Whoa—you're already dressed and ready to go. Where?"

"I have to buy a dress for tonight. Sergei doesn't want the waitresses wearing our usual uniforms." She walked farther into the room, swinging a pair of sandals from her fingers.

"Yeah, I'll bet he doesn't. You need to be careful tonight, Britt. This is a party for the Belkins' associates to meet young, accommodating ladies working for the Belkins."

"Well, I'm not accommodating." She tripped to a stop and dropped one of her sandals, red flags flying in her cheeks. "I mean, I won't be accommodating to any of Sergei's friends."

He cleared his throat. "I hope you have a choice. I'm going to be doing my own thing there and might not have a chance to look out for you."

She snatched the sandal up from the carpet. "I can handle myself."

He had no doubt Britt could handle herself under normal circumstances, but the Belkins were anything but normal. He didn't want her slipping away from him.

"Can we meet for lunch and discuss that… strategy?"

Steadying herself with one hand on the credenza, she shoved a sandal onto her right foot and, like a stork, switched to her other leg to put on the left. "All right. I'll be in the area since I'm going to take advantage of shopping in Beverly Hills while I'm here." She dropped her cell phone in her purse. "Should we pick a time and place now since you don't want me calling your phone?"

She made that security measure sound… bad. Maybe it was best he'd raised her prickly side and she'd decided to keep him at arm's length. It would make leaving her so much easier. "Patio of The Ivy at noon."

"See you there." She left the room with a flourish and a cloud of floral perfume.

Alexei blew out a breath and dropped the blanket to the floor. Teaming up with a woman was a lot different from working with his

SEAL team members. He sneezed. None of them wore perfume, for one thing—at least not that he knew of.

He yanked his phone off its charger and thumbed through the messages. What he wouldn't give to have one of his buddies here. He'd even take Slade Gallagher.

He strode into the bedroom and glanced at the tumbled bedclothes. Had she had a restless night, too? He fell across the bed, dragging a pillow over his face. He inhaled the same scent that was floating around the sitting room right now—sweet, feminine, desirable. Closing his eyes, he pictured Britt in the shower, water beading on her soft skin, her lips parted as he skimmed his hands across her body.

The vision gave him an instant erection, and he shoved off the bed and headed toward the shower. He needed a cold one if he hoped to maintain his resistance to Britt Jansen's considerable charms.

LATER THAT DAY, Alexei sat across the table from Britt as she toyed with her salad. "I ended up spending too much money, but at least I can wear the dress again."

"It's not too—" Alexei waved his fork in the air "—sexy, is it?"

She wrinkled her nose and stabbed at a tomato. "It's a little black dress, elegant."

"I'm sure that's not what Sergei had in mind, but good for you. You don't want to be mistaken for anything other than a waitress."

"I don't plan on it. Do you know the layout of the banquet hall?"

Alexei tapped his phone on the table next to his plate. "There's a Russian restaurant in the front. The restaurant is separated from the banquet hall by a foyer or anteroom with restrooms. There's a stage in the hall, tables and chairs and private rooms off the main area, down a hallway."

"Are those actual pictures?" She jabbed at his phone with her finger. "Have you been there?"

"I found some pictures of it online and downloaded them, although maybe it will be set up differently for this event." He took a sip of icc water. "I'll be assessing the guests, but mostly I'm going to ingratiate myself with one guest in particular—a supposed arms dealer. I'll also be getting on Sergei's good side."

"Is Sergei really involved in the—" she ducked her head and looked both ways "—terrorist activities? Somehow I just can't picture him hobnobbing with committed terrorists."

"You're probably right. I can't imagine old

Olav Belkin would trust his son with operations of that magnitude. That's what makes Sergei ripe fruit for plucking. He's a fool."

"You don't think the FBI has already tried plucking that particular fruit?" She hunched forward, burying her chin in her hand. "It *is* the FBI that would handle a crime family like the Belkins, isn't it? Or are you already working with the FBI? You never really told me how a navy SEAL sniper wound up in LA."

And he wasn't planning on it now. He didn't want to scare her off at this point—or maybe he did. If she knew the truth, she might back off, go home.

He shrugged and picked up the second half of his burger. "I can't tell you that."

"Not sure why." She narrowed her green eyes. "It's not like I'm going to reveal secrets to the press or anything. I'm assuming you haven't told the agencies involved in this about me."

Chewing slowly, he placed his burger back on the plate. He slid the napkin from his lap and wiped his mouth and then his hands, folded it over and positioned it next to his plate.

Britt's gaze tracked his every movement. "Well, have you?"

"I have not."

"I didn't think so." She flipped her hair back from her face. "You'd be in a world of trouble if they found out, wouldn't you?"

A muscle ticked at the corner of his mouth. "I'm going to be in a world of trouble anyway."

"What do you mean? I'm not going to rat you out." She ran her fingertip across the seam of her lips. "If you help me find out what happened to Leanna, even if you don't, nobody will ever hear a peep out of me. W-we can pretend we never met."

He toyed with the edge of the napkin. "It's not about you, Britt."

"I don't get it. Why are you going to be in trouble?" She tilted her head to the side, and her golden hair slid over one shoulder.

"Because I'm not working with an agency. I don't have much of a plan, and I don't have any backup...except you."

He closed one eye, formed his fingers into a gun and aimed it over Britt's shoulder. "I just want to kill Olav Belkin."

ALEXEI'S WHISPERED WORDS sent a chill racing up Britt's spine, and she gripped the edge of the table. Oh God, she was sitting across from a maniac.

"I… You… Who are you?" She half rose out of her chair and then thumped back down.

He covered one of her hands with his, and if she'd given in to her first instinct, she would've snatched it away. But Alexei's hand felt warm, secure. He'd protected her, kept her safe…and lied to her.

"I'm Alexei Ivanov, US Navy SEAL sniper. That's all still true, but I'm also the son of Aleksandr Ivanov, who was murdered by Olav Belkin, and I'm here to avenge that murder."

She licked her dry lips and sucked down some iced tea through her straw. "So, there's no connection between the Belkins and terrorists? You're just trying to get close enough to Belkin to…kill him?"

"There is a connection. The Belkins have worked with terrorists before, in Russia. It's not new territory for them. If I can take down Olav Belkin, his terrorist connections will run scared." He spread his hands. "It's a win-win."

"Except what you're doing is illegal. If you're caught, it will end your career, regardless of the favor you're doing the world." She grabbed his hand, digging her nails into his skin. "Is your vengeance worth that? Everything you worked so hard to achieve?"

His gaze dropped to his hand in her possession. "You know, I never even met my father.

My mother was pregnant when my father was murdered, and I was born in New York after relatives got her out of Russia."

"How did it happen?" Maybe if she could get him to talk about it matter-of-factly, putting his Russian passion aside… "How did your father know Belkin, or was it random?"

His head jerked when the waitress showed up to take their plates. "Anything else?"

"Coffee for both of us." Britt wagged her finger between herself and Alexei.

He shoved his dark hair back from his face with one hand. "It wasn't random. My father was a shopkeeper in Saint Petersburg. Belkin was a member of the *Vory v Zakone*."

Britt raised her eyebrows. "The what?"

"*Vory v Zakone*. The Russian mob in the old Soviet Union. It literally means 'thieves in law.' They were involved in all criminal activities—drugs, girls, extortion. And my father " he lifted one shoulder in that very Russian manner of his "—objected to those activities. The *Vory* answered his objections by slitting his throat one night in his shop."

Britt covered her mouth with both hands. No wonder Alexei wanted revenge. She'd been ready to do violence against Sergei for lying about her sister, and she didn't even know if he was involved in Leanna's disappearance yet.

"That's awful. I mean, I have no words, really." She pressed her lips together when the waitress returned with their coffee.

Alexei dumped some sugar in his coffee with a shaky hand, his jaw tight.

So much for tamping down that Russian temper.

"Alexei." Britt stirred some cream into her cup. "What did your father want for you?"

"Are you going to psychoanalyze me?" His lips twisted. "No need."

"Would your father want you to avenge his death at the risk of your own future? What about your mother? She left the Soviet Union, raised you here away from all that, away from the old grudges."

"I had my chance once." Alexei held his coffee cup aloft and stared over the rim into the distance, into some other time and place. "I had an opportunity to take out Belkin, had him in my sights."

"What stopped you?"

"Duty and country. I had a different assignment at the time. I completed the assignment, and shooting Belkin at that point would've compromised everything, compromised the safety of my teammates."

"And now?"

"I'm on my own."

"What is your official reason for being in LA?"

"I don't have an official reason. I'm on leave between deployments."

"Your…unit…" She waved her hand in the air. "The navy doesn't know where you are?"

"They know I'm vacationing in LA."

She drove the heel of her hand against her forehead. "You can't do this, Alexei. I won't let you. You'll destroy everything you've worked for."

"On the contrary, this is everything I've been working for. The terrorist group Belkin is courting is one controlled by someone my team has been after for a very long time. Someone who captured and tortured one of my teammates." He snapped his fingers. "Like I said, a win-win for everyone."

"Except you." She ran her finger along the rim of her cup. "Is your mother still around?"

He threw her a sharp glance. "She lives in Florida with her second husband."

"And how do you think she'd feel if you were arrested for murder? Court-martialed? She must be extremely proud of her navy SEAL son."

"You—" he leveled a finger at her "—don't play fair. Is this how you beat your clients into submission?"

She folded both of her hands around one of his. "Think about it. Think about her. Do you really believe she wants you to revisit those old hurts from the old country?"

"It's not right." The corner of his eye twitched, and his hand in her possession clenched into a fist. "My father tried to do the right thing, and not only was he murdered for it, the police did nothing to bring his killers to justice."

"Paid off?"

"Paid off and scared. The *Vory v Zakone* controlled that whole area. That's why my mom had to get out."

"I understand that thirst for revenge. Why do you think I basically gave up my life in Charlotte to come out here? I want to find out what happened to my sister, I want the people who threatened her, the people who killed Jerome, to be punished, but there are ways—legal ways."

Alexei snorted and disentangled his hand from hers. "Legal means are useless against people like this. Didn't you discover that already with your sister?"

"What you and your team of snipers do is legal. You don't run off and go rogue...do you?"

"We can't. It would get us a court-martial."

She smacked the table. "Exactly. Don't do this, Alexei. Your sense of satisfaction will be short-lived, and if the authorities figure out who killed Belkin, your career will be over. You'd be hurting so many people—your mother, your teammates…me."

His gaze jumped to her face. "I never want to hurt you, Britt."

The heat sparking from his eyes melted her insides. Even if she couldn't have this man, she wanted to know he was free and doing the job he was supposed to do.

She spread her hands on the table, her two thumbs meeting. "It would hurt me to know that you were in some military prison serving time for killing that dirtbag Belkin. There has to be another way."

Alexei pinged his fingernail against his coffee cup. "Maybe if I can get some serious evidence that Belkin is working with Vlad, the task force will give me the go-ahead to pursue the investigation."

"Wait. What?" She tucked her hair behind one ear. "Who's Vlad and what task force?"

"Vlad is an enemy sniper. We don't know what nationality he is, but he uses a Russian sniper rifle—just like mine. We've been tracking his activities for a few years. He graduated from his sniper-for-hire activities to forming his own terrorist network. So far, we've been able to thwart his plans in the US."

"He's plotting attacks here? And this is the person the Belkins are dealing with?"

"We think so. He tried hooking up with a Colombian cartel, but we were able to quash that. This is obviously his next effort to expand his operations in the US."

"There's a task force to bring him down?"

"Exclusively dedicated to the goal. Some of my teammates were assigned to the task force at various times in the past several months." He shrugged. "The Belkin crime family connection is just chatter at this point."

"But if you can prove it, you might get the go-ahead from this task force to investigate?"

"That's what I'm thinking. It's not—" He drummed his fingers on the table. "This task force is not a typical one. Navy SEALs were called back to the States to perform operations under the radar. Much of what they did was out of the bounds of law enforcement or military justice."

She swirled the coffee in her cup, a smile creeping to her lips. "Sounds right up your alley. What do you need to do to make this happen?"

His brows collided over his nose. "Even if I find the proof of the Belkin-Vlad connection, I might not be the task force's first choice to lead the charge. They know my background."

"Would make perfect sense to me. Who better to infiltrate the Belkin operation than a Russian American who speaks the language?"

"There is something to that. It seems like my teammates were chosen for their specific assignments because of their connections to the people involved. The task force leader, Ariel, is not your typical CIA policy wonk."

"Ariel?" Britt sucked in her bottom lip. "That's who you were emailing before. I thought she might be your girlfriend."

"Honestly, I'm not even sure she's a girl, and I never sent that email."

"Aha!" She wriggled in her chair. "So, you had already thought about contacting the task force."

"It had crossed my mind."

Britt pulled her phone closer and checked the time. "Then we both know what we have to do tonight—you need to find evidence of Vlad, and I need to find clues about Leanna."

"Just be careful. I think you have an idea of whom you're dealing with now."

"I pretty much knew that from the beginning."

The real surprise had been the confession

of Alexei Ivanov—a story worthy of a Russian novel with betrayal, vengeance and redemption.

She just had to make sure this story didn't feature a doomed love affair.

Chapter Ten

Britt studied Alexei as he faced the full-length mirror in the hotel room, picking an imaginary speck of lint from his impeccably tailored jacket.

"I do have one question for you." She smoothed the skirt of her black dress over her thighs. "If the government is not sponsoring and paying for your so-called vacation in LA, where is all the cash coming from for the fancy crib and threads?"

"Crib and threads?" He cracked a rare smile and then patted the pocket of his jacket. "Self funded."

She leaned into the mirror next to him, dabbing at her lipstick. "I didn't realize the navy paid so well—even for hotshots like you."

"After my mother moved to the States and had me, she met a very wealthy Russian businessman. The man, my stepfather, treated me like a son and gave me everything I wanted—still does. I have a half sister, and they treat her like a princess. I think she even pretends she's a Russian princess." He rolled his eyes.

"Does your stepfather know what you're doing out here?"

"No. He'd tell my mother. This—" he swept his hand across the suite "—is all from my trust fund, which I rarely touch."

"Would your stepfather approve of what you're doing? Or what you were *going* to do?"

"Approve? No, because it would upset my mother, but he'd understand. He comes from that same world, and that's why he left. All business was controlled by the *Vory,* and after the fall of the Soviet Union, the oligarchs moved in to claim the spoils. Maks chafed under the restrictions and the graft and became a self-made billionaire here."

"After tonight, it won't come to that." She bumped him with her hip. "Move it, Russki. You're primping more than I am."

"You don't need to primp." He pinched the hem of her dress between two fingers, rubbing them together. "You look beautiful."

Alexei's compliments were simple, straightforward and gave her a warm glow inside because she knew they were sincere.

"You look beautiful, too." She spun away

from the mirror to face him and smoothed her hands against the lapels of his jacket. A pulse throbbed deep in her belly, and she kissed his mouth. He couldn't possibly blame her for that, as his lips were inches from hers and she never did have much self-control.

His eyes flickered but he didn't back away from her. "Remember our signal if you're in trouble?"

"I'm going to twist my hair around one hand. Don't worry. I'm going to be fine. This is a party in a banquet hall behind a restaurant. I'm going to be serving drinks and Russian caviar."

"Just don't forget what this party is all about." He touched a finger to her nose. "Despite what Sergei may have told you or even the other waitresses, this is a gathering of wealthy men and the desperate young women who are bound to serve them."

Britt shivered. "It makes me sick. Leanna must've been livid when she found out what was going on."

"Don't make the same mistake she did. Don't show your hand."

"You either, Mikhail Orloff." She tugged on his lapels. "How are you getting to the party? You're not riding the motorcycle in this getup, are you?"

"Town car."

"Fancy. I have to drive over in my old clunker."

"Just be careful."

"You said that already."

"Can't be said enough."

She held up a hand. "Okay, I'm leaving. I'll see you over there, and I *will* be careful."

She slung her bag over her shoulder, and as she reached the door, Alexei's stride ate up the space between them.

He grabbed her shoulders and planted a kiss on her that totally messed up her makeup—and damn, she didn't even care.

Forty minutes later, Britt pulled up in front of Eastern Nights, the Belkins' flagship restaurant. A valet parking attendant rushed to her window.

She flashed him a smile. "I'm the help. Where do we park?"

"Pull around the corner, and park in the lot behind the restaurant." He waved his arm behind him.

She parked her car and then stood beside it to wait for two of the other waitresses as they pulled into a parking space.

One of the women, Theanessa, rubbed her hands as she approached Britt. "Get ready for some great tips tonight."

Britt nodded. The only tip she wanted was the one that would lead her to Leanna.

As they all pushed through the back door of the restaurant, Britt asked, "Are the dancers going to be putting on a show tonight?"

Theanessa smirked. "Hell no. This party's supposed to be a little higher class than that. There's a band, some dancing—not the topless kind—and it's mix and mingle for Sergei's friends and some special ladies."

The other waitress nudged Britt with her elbow and whispered in her ear. "High-class escorts."

"Oh." She put a hand to her throat. "But we're just serving drinks and appetizers, right?"

"You're not a guest, girl." Theanessa shed her sweater to reveal a low-cut red dress. "We get our minimum wage plus tips. Those escorts are making the big bucks."

Britt bit her bottom lip. She doubted the escorts, as Theanessa called them, were getting paid at all if they were part of the Belkins' stable.

She blew out a breath. "Well, I'm just here to be a waitress because Jessie pulled out. Do either of you know what happened to Jessie? I haven't seen her for a few days."

"Nope." Theanessa gave the other waitress

a little push from behind. "The Tattle-Tale has a high turnover."

Britt slid a glance to the other woman, whose name she couldn't remember. Had she been about to spill the beans on Jessie? Britt would have to get her alone tonight for a few discreet questions.

That was all she was here for—discreet questions.

When all the waitresses had arrived, they gathered around Irina for instructions.

Irina, still wearing her yoga pants and over-size blouse, clapped her hands. "All right. Guests begin arriving in about ten minutes. Pick up trays of vodka and wine and work crowd with those. If someone wants mixed drink, they go to bar unless you want to get it for them. You pick up trays of appetizers in the restaurant's kitchen. Any questions?"

One of the waitresses raised her hand. "H-how will the guests know we're not... guests since there's no uniform for tonight?"

Britt laced her fingers in front of her and studied Irina's face. Everyone seemed to know what this party was all about. Would Irina acknowledge that now?

The older woman crooked her finger, and one of the busboys approached the group holding a plastic bin in his arms.

Irina pointed to the floor, and the busboy dropped the bin. She then leaned over and grabbed something from it. A white apron dangled from her fingertips. "You wear these. Then you don't get pretty dresses all dirty."

Britt eased out a sigh. She'd rather wear a frilly white apron than be mistaken for an escort.

Irina tossed out the apron, and Britt caught it with one hand. As she tied it around her waist, Theanessa nudged her back.

"Kinda ruins the effect of our sexy dresses, doesn't it? Why didn't Sergei just have us wear our regular black skirts and white blouses?" She flounced off, dragging the apron behind her on the floor.

The young waitress Britt had met in the parking lot sidled up next to her. "I'm glad we're wearing something that's gonna say we're waitresses and not...hookers."

Britt lodged her tongue in the corner of her mouth as she smoothed the apron over her dress. "Well, they're not exactly hookers, are they? I mean, they're like escorts."

The woman rolled her eyes. "Call it what you want. They're gonna get paid for sex."

"I'm just here to serve drinks and food." Britt lifted her shoulders. "Do you know what happened to Jessie? Sergei said she quit."

"I'm just here to serve drinks and food." The waitress yanked the ties on her apron and turned her back on Britt.

Britt wandered around the room, taking in the orchestra tuning up on the stage and the two bartenders setting up on either side of the large hall. Stepan, Jerome's replacement at the Tattle-Tale, lifted his hand in a wave, and Britt waved back. She just wanted to fit in tonight and not cause any waves.

Maybe once Alexei got his proof of the ties between Belkin and Vlad, she'd go home and leave it up to that task force to find Leanna… or at least tell her what had happened to her sister.

Britt blinked back the tears that tingled in her nose and trailed her hand along the tex-tured paper on the walls. Her hand dropped off at the gap created by a small hallway tucked off the main room.

She poked her head around the corner, not-ing several closed doors. She'd already seen the bathrooms between the restaurant and the banquet hall, so these couldn't be restrooms. She glanced over her shoulder and took a step into the hallway.

One of the doors swung open, and Britt jumped back.

Irina emerged, pursing her lips when she

noticed Britt. Irina bore down on her and grabbed her upper arm, the Russian woman's bony fingers digging into Britt's flesh.

"Nothing here, Barbie. Guests will be arriving soon. Get tray of drinks and get busy."

"Sorry." Britt shook her off. "Just exploring."

"No exploring. Just working."

As Britt walked away, she placed a hand against her pounding heart. Irina had an iron grip—and she was completely loyal to the Belkins…and armed.

Drawing in a deep breath, she squared her shoulders and strode toward Stepan's bar. "Do you have any trays ready yet?"

"Just getting started. You help me?"

"Sure. What do you need?"

He handed her an expensive bottle of vodka, icy cold, and pointed to a tray of shot glasses on the table behind her. "Fill those about three-quarters."

"You got it." She tipped the vodka into glass after glass until they all shimmered with the clear liquid. "Do you want me to do another?"

He gestured toward the entrance, where several people had begun to gather. "Time for one more, and then we get busy."

He set up another tray of glasses for her and lined up two more chilled bottles of vodka.

As she watched a stream of liquid pour into the first shot glass, she asked, "You've worked these parties before?"

"Once."

"Do they get pretty crazy?"

"Crazy?" He laughed. "Not crazy with these boring old men."

She finished off the tray with a flourish. "Well, I hope these boring old men tip well."

"They will." Stepan's gaze tracked down her body.

Britt folded her arms across her chest. "That's what I'm talkin' about. You're on your own now, Stepan. I'm going to start mingling with the vodka."

She hoisted one of the trays and couldn't get out of Stepan's slimy presence fast enough. Since she'd filled that first tray, more guests had arrived and were fanning out across the room to park at tables and wander to the back of the banquet hall to check out the long table, groaning with Russian delicacies.

Britt kept watch for one tall, dark, good-looking Russian with blue eyes, but Alexei hadn't arrived yet. Instead a squat, silver-haired man in the middle of the room held sway over a group of people hanging on to his every word.

She had a visceral reaction to the man, like

a punch to the gut, and had no doubt she was watching Olav Belkin in action.

Stretching her lips into a smile, she approached a cluster of men. "Vodka?"

Two of the group relieved her of two glasses, and she dived into the growing crowd to dispense with the rest. She circled back around to Stepan's station, dropped off the empty tray and picked up one crowded with flutes of champagne.

This cargo gave her a better opportunity to get up close and personal with more of the women guests. She glided up to three men and two women, the women perfectly made up and exquisitely dressed.

"Champagne?" She proffered the tray and almost dropped the whole thing when one of the women reached for a glass, exposing the small, fresh tattoo on the underside of her forearm.

Britt's eyes bounced to the woman's face, and this time the tray wobbled in her hand so much a couple of the flutes tipped over.

Britt grabbed a bunch of napkins from the stack on her tray and blotted the puddle of liquid. "I am so sorry."

"No problems." Mila took another glass and smiled. Then she ducked her head. "You coming to party tomorrow night at Rage, Barbie? Last night for me as dancer."

"Oh, I'll try."

With her pulse racing a mile a minute, Britt scurried back to the bar—not Stepan's—and placed the tray on the table next to it. Wedging her hands on either side of the tray, she leaned forward. Mila had gone through with it. She'd gotten the Belkin tattoo, and now she was here at this party as a commodity. She was moving from dancer to escort.

She squeezed her eyes shut. Mila didn't seem to be here under duress. She'd smiled, taken a glass of champagne, looked beautiful.

"Hey, Barbie, right?"

Britt looked up and met Theanessa's eyes over a tray of food. "Yes."

"If you're between deliveries, can you take this food out there?" She winked. "I have to make a little detour."

Britt shifted her gaze over Theanessa's shoulder, and it collided with an older man's beady black eyes.

His stare hardened, and Britt looked away. Did Theanessa know what she was getting into? Did any of these women?

Reaching out her arms, Britt said, "Sure, sure. I'll take it."

"Thanks."

As Theanessa handed off the tray, Britt grabbed her wrist. "Be careful."

Theanessa's laughter trilled in her throat as she spun away toward her new friend, leaving Britt gripping the heavy tray with two hands, the edges cutting into her palms.

She waded back into the crowd, which had thinned out a bit once the orchestra had struck up its first tune. Several couples claimed the dance floor, the women like colorful butterflies floating closer and closer to the spiders' webs.

Britt spotted Alexei with two other men, heads together. Did he realize Olav Belkin was in the room? Of course he did. He probably had him on his radar at all times.

She zigzagged through the mass of people to reach him and ducked into their circle. "Appetizers?"

"Thanks." Alexei selected blini with smoked salmon from the tray.

One of his companions touched her hip. "I don't know. What's on the menu?"

Britt's smile tightened and she raised the tray close to his face. "Only what's on the tray."

The man guffawed and elbowed the third member of the group in the ribs. "She's feisty. I like feisty."

"Boris." Alexei stepped in front of the man, breaking his contact with Britt. "I want to continue our discussion about that proposition."

"Ah, for a young man, you're too interested in business. You let go a little."

Alexei clapped Boris on the shoulder. "There's plenty of time for pleasure."

Britt took the opportunity to slip away from the group. She brushed past another waitress and snatched a shot glass of vodka from her tray. Without looking one way or the other, Britt downed the vodka in one gulp.

She coughed and dropped the glass onto her own tray, but at least the booze steadied her jangling nerves and shaky hands. She had to get a grip. She couldn't fall apart every time one of these guys made a pass at her. She could always complain to Sergei. From what she understood from the other women, Sergei didn't want any of the waitresses getting any side action. Theanessa was taking her chances.

The night went on in much the same way— fending off a few advances and delivering food and drink, and then mostly drink, to the partygoers. She'd wanted to snatch a few minutes with Alexei but didn't want to raise suspicions.

Apparently Alexei didn't either as Britt

hadn't seen him with Olav once. It must be killing him to be so close to the man who'd murdered his father.

As the action picked up on the dance floor and the waitressing consisted more of collecting empty glasses and plates than delivering anything to the guests, Britt began scoping out the different areas of the banquet hall. While the women were attentive to the male guests, she hadn't witnessed any groping or manhandling. Did they all just go quietly away to hotel rooms?

The hallway at the back of the room where Irina had shooed her away commanded Britt's attention more than once throughout the evening. The movement in that spot was discreet but noticeable.

Her gaze swept the room of preoccupied people, and she meandered toward the hallway, keeping a tray in her hand for appearances' sake. She turned the corner into the hallway quickly and flattened her body against the wall. A door opened, and she placed her tray on the floor and crouched forward as if fixing her shoe.

Through the veil of her hair, she watched as a man exited the room and strolled back to the banquet hall, adjusting his shirt collar.

She wanted to be ready the next time a door

opened, so she continued down the hallway and positioned herself between two of the doors, facing two other doors. Again, she pretended to be fussing with her shoe and left the tray on the floor—just a waitress collecting herself.

Five minutes later, her patience was rewarded as the door across the hall opened, the glow from the room creating a rectangle of light on the carpet. She shifted away from the light.

The man at the door spit out something in Russian, clearly angry. A woman responded, and Britt recognized Irina's voice. She jerked her head up to peer into the room and clapped a hand over her mouth.

Irina sat on the edge of a bed where Jessie, wearing lacy lingerie, was sprawled out. She looked dead—no, drugged—her head rolling to one side and her arm sweeping the floor where it hung off the bed.

Britt braced her hand against the wall to push to her feet. She began to careen toward the open door. She had to save Jessie. She had to protect Leanna.

Before she could take one more step, a rough hand clamped over her mouth from behind, jerking her back, lifting her off her feet and dragging her toward the exit.

She clawed at the fingers restricting her air and arched her body, but her actions were futile.

Maybe she'd find Leanna after all.

Chapter Eleven

The man's words came at him in a fog, and Alexei dragged his gaze away from the hallway where Britt had disappeared several minutes ago with an empty tray.

He had an idea what went on back there, and she had no business in that vicinity.

Holding up a hand to his companion, he said, "Excuse me, David. A girl I've had my eye on all night is finally alone. I'm going to try my luck."

"Go, go, man. Enjoy yourself."

Alexei cut through the crowd, making a beeline for the dark hallway. As he took the corner, a door slammed, but another opened in the back. From studying the layout beforehand, Alexei knew that door led to the parking lot behind the banquet.

The darkness obscured his vision, but he

could make out two figures going through that door—and one was struggling.

Alexei jogged down the hallway, his adrenaline spiking when he saw the empty tray on the floor.

He burst through the exit door, and the weak light affixed to the back of the building shed a yellow glow over a man choking Britt.

Ice-cold rage ran through his body, and he launched forward, grabbing the man by the back of the neck. Alexei yanked him off Britt and shook him like a rag doll, the toes of the man's shoes scuffing the asphalt.

Alexei squeezed the man's carotid artery, and he went limp in his grasp.

Britt had scrambled to her feet and grabbed Alexei's arm. "He's out. Let him go."

He dropped the man and he fell in a heap. Then he stepped over the man's prone form and pulled Britt into his arms. "Are you all right? Did he hurt you?"

"He choked me." She stroked her throat. "If you hadn't come out here, I don't know what he would've done. How did you know? What were you doing in that hallway?"

"I've had my eye on you all night, *moya solnishka.*" He smoothed her hair from her flushed face. "When you didn't emerge from that hallway, I knew something had gone wrong."

"I'm glad you did. I guess that secret sign we discussed doesn't work if you're out of sight." She drove her forehead against his chest. "I—I saw Jessie in one of those rooms. You know, the waitress who auditioned for Sergei. Alexei, she looked drugged. Completely out of it."

He wrapped his arms around her tighter, wanting to protect her from all the ugliness in that place. "You know what those rooms are used for?"

"I didn't think the couples would be hooking up right here. I figured they'd leave for a hotel room or something."

"If the men want a taste before they buy, that's where they do it."

She pushed away from him and staggered backward. "I think I'm going to be sick. Why Jessie?"

"Maybe Sergei thought she understood what it meant to be a dancer, and when she balked, he took other measures." He crouched next to the fallen man and shoved up one of his eyelids. "We need to get out of here before this guy comes to."

"What are we going to do? Where are we going to go?"

"Who else was in the room with Jessie?"

"Some Russian man and Irina."

"Did they see you?"

"I don't know. I don't think so. The door was swinging closed again right when I saw Jessie on the bed and that—" she aimed a toe at the unconscious man "—goon came up behind me."

"So, right now only the three of us know you were in that hallway and saw Jessie. This guy—" he went further than Britt and kicked the man in the side "—doesn't even know what you saw."

"What does that mean?"

"It means we're going back inside and pretending nothing happened." He took her by the shoulders and turned her to face the building. "You go first. Grab your tray, and get back to work. If you see Irina, act normal."

"That's going to be hard to do." Turning to face him, she circled her throat with her fingers.

"You can do it, Britt. Put that poker face you use with your clients into action."

"What are you going to do? We have to save Jessie. I think the man in the room was angry because she was nonresponsive. We have to get her out of there."

"Right now, I'm going around the front, and I'm going to bum a cigarette from someone, as if I went out there for a smoke." He pinched her chin. "I'll think of some way to get Jessie out."

"And Mila. The dancer who had the tattoo artist's card. She's here tonight—with the Belkin family tattoo on her arm."

"We can't save them all, Britt, at least not until the entire operation is brought down."

"Tatyana's baby. The woman who called me said finding that baby would bring them all down."

"So will linking the Belkins to Vlad's terrorist network."

She gathered the front of his shirt in her hands. "Are you any closer? Did you find something?"

"I might have."

"You saw Olav Belkin tonight, didn't you?"

"I did. How did you know him?"

"He was easy to spot."

Alexei clenched his teeth. It had taken all his self-control not to haul off and punch the old man in the face. And if he'd had a gun with him...? But he'd never planned to take Belkin out in public like this. Just a well-placed bullet from a great, great distance.

He shook his head. Britt had been right. What would that achieve except for slaking his thirst for revenge?

Taking her hand, he said, "Let's see the

rest of this night out. The man who attacked you might not be so willing to tell anyone what happened. The Belkins are unforgiving bosses. The fact that this SOB landed out in the parking lot facedown would not bode well for him with the Belkins."

"Okay." Britt pulled in a deep breath and straightened her frilly apron.

He squeezed her hand before letting her go. "Do not stop by that room or any of those rooms. Get your tray and go."

She turned at the door and mouthed the words *thank you*.

Brushing off his jacket, Alexei took off for the front of the restaurant. He stepped over a row of bushes to change his direction and make it look like he was coming from the restaurant's front door.

He joined a group of men smoking and chatting. "Does someone have a cigarette? I'm trying to quit, but you know how that goes."

"I'm gonna quit at the end of the summer. I promised my wife." The man shoved a half-empty pack of smokes and a matchbook into Alexei's hand. "Keep 'em."

"Thanks." Alexei put a cigarette between his lips and struck a match from the Eastern Nights matchbook and lit it. He tucked the matches into the front pocket of his jacket, an idea forming in his head.

The group broke apart, and some of the men left and others wandered back into the party. Alexei followed them, tossing his unsmoked cigarette to the ground and crushing it beneath the toe of his shoe.

Once inside, he scanned the room and let out a breath when he spotted Britt carrying a tray of empty glasses to the kitchen. His contact had already left for the evening, more interested in business than pleasure, so Alexei didn't know many of the people left—except the Belkins, including Sergei. He'd been able to get the measure of the man…and the man had been lacking.

Olav still held court in a corner of the room, relaxing on a deep sofa, two young, gorgeous women on either side of him. If Alexei had his rifle with him, it would be so easy to take Belkin out right now. Then it would be lifted—this burden he carried. Of course, he'd probably be dead before his bullet hit Belkin. And Britt would be on her own.

There was another way, but Alexei didn't want Belkin to get off again by agreeing to work with the FBI to nail Vlad. Alexei wouldn't allow that to happen—not this time.

He moved into the anteroom between the

restaurant and the banquet hall and nodded at a couple of women walking arm in arm to the restrooms.

He stood in front of a painting of the Black Sea and then reached into his pocket for the book of matches. He struck one, and pinching it between his thumb and forefinger, he held it up to the sprinkler head.

A small curl of smoke kissed the edge of the sprinkler, and it sputtered to life. Water splattered against the painting and, in a chain reaction, set off the other sprinkler heads in the foyer.

Then Alexei poked his head into the kitchen, where several busboys were washing and stacking dishes. He yelled, "Fire! Get out!"

The busboys looked at each other, and Alexei shouted, *"Fuego!"*

They dropped the dishes and crowded out of the kitchen.

When they'd all left, Alexei held a match to another sprinkler head and pulled the fire alarm by the stoves. As the alarm wailed, he smiled to himself. "That should do it."

By the time he returned to the banquet hall, chaos reigned. The sprinklers had gone off in the hall, also. Women screamed and held their hands over their heads to protect their hair and makeup from the relentless streams of water.

Sergei charged through the room, waving his hands and yelling, "No fire department. No police."

Sergei's words just caused more panic as the men with hookers on their arms either disengaged themselves or ran for the doors, dragging their newfound companions along with them.

Alexei's gaze darted among the pandemonium until it rested on Britt at the entrance to the hallway. Their eyes met, and he shook his head.

He threaded his way through the agitated guests to reach Britt. "Leave now. Check in with Irina, if you want. I'll knock on those doors and sound the alarm."

Just then, the bartender who wasn't Stepan rushed past them and saved Alexei the trouble. He banged on each door and shouted in Russian, "Get out. Get the girls out now. Police coming."

Alexei nudged Britt. "There you go. It's over."

"I'd kiss you right now, but I don't want to raise any eyebrows." She kissed her fingers instead and pressed them to his throat. Then she joined the herd of people making their way to the exits.

Alexei edged along the walls of the room until he came up behind the sitting area where Olav had stationed himself throughout the party with his inner circle.

Someone had left a jacket draped across one of the chairs. Alexei grabbed it and felt the pockets. Bingo. He slipped the cell phone from the jacket's pocket and dropped it into his own. He was starting his own collection.

He tented the abandoned jacket over his head and made for the nearest exit just as the first set of fire trucks rolled onto the scene. The firefighters wouldn't find a fire or even a faulty sprinkler system, and they sure as hell wouldn't find any evidence of a party for rich men and a bevy of beautiful escorts.

Alexei had made out a lot better. He'd found a couple of cell phones, had made contact with a weapons dealer and had gained Sergei Belkin's trust.

But more important than any of that? He'd saved Britt from a thug's attack.

An hour later, Alexei joined Britt in the hotel room, stretched out on the sofa, watching TV with her laptop beside her.

He shrugged out of his jacket and sat in the chair across from her, hunching forward on his knees. "Nobody approached you tonight about the attack in the hallway?"

"No. Sergei's minion must've been too embarrassed to tell his boss someone had gotten the better of him."

"But he's going to tell him you saw Jessie in that room. Somehow, he'll get word to Sergei that he saw you in the hallway and you ran away—something to protect himself but implicate you. He's most likely a loyal drone."

Britt drew her knees to her chest and wrapped her arms around her legs. "I can talk my way out of it, just like I did with the towing receipt."

He launched out of the chair and knelt beside the sofa. "No, you can't. You saw Jessie in a room, drugged, noncompliant. Are you going to convince Sergei you don't care about that?"

"I can pretend I didn't see anything. How best to prove that by coming into work like nothing happened? If I bail now, Sergei's going to know for sure I saw something." She rested a hand on the back of his neck. "It would be my word against the man's who attacked me."

"Exactly. Why would Sergei believe some waitress he just hired over a loyal foot soldier? And about that foot soldier, he's going to find it strange that you didn't report the assault. Why wouldn't you, unless you knew you'd seen something you shouldn't have seen."

"What's the guy going to do? Approach me and ask why I didn't tell on him?" Her fingers wiggled into his hair. "I've never seen him before anyway. There were lots of waitresses there that night, many of them in black dresses. It was dark in the hallway, and he came at me from behind. He probably never even saw my face."

He closed his eyes, trying not to be swayed by the gentle fingers massaging his scalp. "You have a hundred and one reasons not to go back to the Tattle-Tale."

"I'm not going back tomorrow, anyway. I finally have a day off."

"Good."

"And you? Do you think you have enough information for the Vlad task force to get put on this assignment officially?"

"I think I do. I met a man at the party who's an arms dealer. If Belkin is partnering with terrorists, it will involve weapons, most likely in exchange for drugs—pure opium from Afghanistan. It's another inroad, and I'm going to contact Ariel about it."

"I'm glad." She dragged her fingers through

his hair and brushed his cheek with her knuckles. "That was a crazy idea you had."

Grabbing her wrist, he snorted. "My idea was crazy? And your idea about infiltrating the Russian mob to find your sister was perfectly sane."

"I didn't know Leanna was involved with the Russian mob until you told me. I just thought it was something straightforward, like an affair with her boss." Britt let loose with a long sigh. "I wish it had been so simple. Ever since I saw Jessie in that room, I've had a cold fear in my belly about Leanna."

He pressed his lips against the inside of her wrist. "You're afraid she might've wound up like Jessie."

"Do you think it's possible?" She slid her legs off the sofa and dug her elbows into her thighs. "I thought the Belkins only wanted young women from Russia, women cut off from their families, alone, desperate. That's not Jessie. She must've done something, said something during that audition that set Sergei off."

"The Belkins are capable of anything." Alexei rose to his feet and stretched. "It's been another long night. Get to bed, and we'll debrief tomorrow."

"I don't think I ever thanked you." She

stood up beside him and curled her arms around his waist. "You saved me from that man and then you saved Jessie and probably a few other women by setting off the sprinklers."

"I didn't save those other women, Britt. They won't be saved until the Belkin crime family is stopped."

"Bring them all down." She tapped her lower lip. "Find Tatyana's baby."

"I'll leave that to you. I'm going to track down these weapons and see if I can discover the link between the Belkins and Vlad." He gripped her shoulders and took a step back, away from her aura that seemed to swirl around him. "Get some sleep."

She dropped her hands, releasing him. "What are you afraid of, Alexei?"

"I'm afraid of leaving you."

She blinked. "People have been leaving me all my life—my father, my mother, my sister. You're the surest thing I've had in a long time."

Her words made his heart hurt, and he reached for her again. "Your father's family took you in."

"Oh, yeah." She gave him a little wobbly smile. "Took me away from my baby sister, whom I'd been protecting since she was born, plopped me into the middle of some perfect family that always regarded me as the junkie's kid. My uncle Jason took me in because he thought it was his duty, but he never loved me. And his wife?"

"I'm sorry. I didn't realize that's how it was for you."

"Don't get me wrong." She placed her palms on his chest. "I was grateful for what they did. They were generous with their money, put me through school and wanted to pay for graduate school, but I refused that. They just weren't so generous with their love."

She unbuttoned the top buttons of his shirt and slid her hands inside, splaying her fingers against his bare skin. Her touch scorched him, and he ached with wanting her.

She leaned in, her voice low and husky. "We have a connection. If we explore that connection for one night or two or eight and then you have to leave me, I'll consider myself blessed, not abandoned."

"Anything can happen, *moya solnishka*."

"I know." She grabbed the hem of her dress and pulled it up and over her head. She dropped it in a heap at her feet. "And I've been meaning to ask you, what does *moya solnishka* mean?"

He ran a hand through the blond strands of her hair. "'My sunshine.'"

Her luscious lips curved into a smile. "Then let me be your sunshine—even if it's for one night."

Chapter Twelve

Britt hung on to the heavy arm draped around her waist from behind. For being a reluctant lover, Alexei had taken to the task like a champ.

Stretching her legs, she wiggled her toes against his feet. She'd lied to Alexei. This one night or two or eight with him would never be enough, but she'd never tell him that.

If he believed he could be a better navy SEAL if he had nobody waiting for him, counting on him, loving him, she had to let him have that—even if he was wrong.

His father had been taken from his pregnant mother for doing the right thing, but fate didn't always twist that way.

His breath warmed the back of her neck as he sighed.

She wriggled around to face him and watched him wake up. Would he recoil in regret once it sank in that he'd succumbed to his desires? Their desires?

He peeled open one eye and ran the pad of his thumb over a lock of her hair across her breast. *"Moya solnishka."*

That answered that.

Cuddling into his chest, she said, "That's not fair. I want a cool Russian nickname for you."

"I like Russki, especially when you say it with that bad Russian accent."

She laughed and then felt guilty as hell. What right did she have to be lying in this sumptuous bed with this sumptuous man when Leanna was God knew where? The same feeling had poked her each time she'd scored a goal in soccer or had gone on vacation or attended the prom. What right did she have to be happy when her sister had been stuck with some foster family?

Alexei stroked her back from her neck to her derriere, resting his hand on the curve of her bottom. "What's wrong?"

"Here I am, living it up in a swanky Beverly Hills hotel with a hot guy in my bed, and my sister's still missing."

"And you should be doing what exactly that you aren't already doing? You've put your life in danger countless times to find her."

He pulled her closer, hooking one leg over hers. "You're doing enough, Britt. It's not your fault your father's people didn't want to take in Leanna."

How many times had her own therapist told her that? But when Alexei told her the same thing with his arms tightly wrapped around her, his breath hot in her hair, his hands caressing her flesh—she almost believed it.

She sniffled and rubbed her nose against his shoulder. "Speaking of taking on unrealistic burdens, are you going to contact the task force this morning with your findings and proposition?"

"Yeah." He rolled onto his back and crossed his arms behind his head. "I'm almost afraid to."

"Because you think they'll tell you to stand down and they'll send someone else out here to finish the task?"

"That about sums it up."

"Then you have to let it go and trust others to do the job."

Twisting his head to the side, he said, "Even if those others aren't going to look into the sex trafficking and find out what happened to Leanna?"

She swallowed hard. Alexei had nailed it. If the people in charge told him to back away from the Belkins, she might never be able to track down Leanna. She had no illusions that she could go up against the Belkins herself, even if she found evidence that they'd... harmed Leanna. Even if she found that baby. Tatyana's baby.

He nudged her head with his elbow. "Even then?"

"Even then. Maybe you could put in a word about the trafficking, about the baby."

"Back to the baby." He kissed the top of her head and then rolled out of the bed.

"You didn't hear this woman on the phone. She sounded so sure of herself."

"We don't even know who called you. Did anyone give you any hints last night? Wink at you? Try to get you alone?"

"Only Stepan."

Alexei stopped in midstretch. "What does that mean?"

"Don't worry. It's not just me. He's interested in all the ladies."

"I wonder how much he knows about what's going on."

"You planning on finding out?"

"Could be a good resource. A lot of times these low-level disgruntled drones are ripe for turning on their bosses."

"Not sure I'd call Stepan one of those, but do you know who else I want to talk to?"

"I'm afraid to ask."

"Calvin, the homeless guy who hangs out near the Tattle-Tale. He obviously knows Leanna. Maybe he saw something. Maybe she told him something."

"You'd better not be caught talking to him near the club. Irina already saw you two together. She might get suspicious."

"Maybe I can lure him away with the promise of lunch."

"Just be careful."

"Can I lure you out with the promise of breakfast?" Stretching out her arms for him, she scooted to the edge of the bed.

Grabbing her hands, he pulled her to her feet and against his body. "Only if I can lure you into the shower first."

She bared her teeth against his collarbone. "This hard body is the only lure I need."

And just like that, Alexei made her forget everything for several blissful moments—but not before she said a silent apology to Leanna and a prayer.

After breakfast, Britt watched Alexei zoom off on his motorcycle while she finished her coffee at the outdoor café on Sunset.

The baby in the stroller at the table next to

hers gurgled and waved his sticky hand in her direction. She wiggled her fingers in response, and he rewarded her with a toothless smile. She melted just a little bit inside.

"He likes you." Mom dabbed a trail of drool from the baby's chin. "Do you and your husband have any children?"

Britt raised her eyebrows. "My husband?"

"Oh." The woman glanced at the chair Alexei had vacated. "Sorry."

"He's my..." Britt waved her hand in the general direction of the empty chair. "...boyfriend."

A rush of heat swept from her chest to her hairline. Why had she lied? She *had* slept with Alexei. That had to qualify as boyfriend status—if just for the day.

"That makes sense since the two of you still seem like you're in that goo-goo-eyed stage."

The warmth of Britt's face deepened. If a stranger could figure out the way she felt toward Alexei, the man himself must be wondering what he could do to extricate himself from her...goo-goo eyes.

The woman's friend returned to the table to save Britt any further embarrassment.

As the women gathered their things, Britt studied the baby. She needed to find a baby of her own. She waved at the little guy again as his mother pushed the stroller onto the sidewalk.

Why had the mysterious caller told Britt to find Tatyana's baby? How did one lose a baby in the first place? The woman hadn't mentioned finding Tatyana, just the baby. That seemed to indicate mom and baby weren't together.

How could a mother be separated from her newborn baby? Britt's hand tightened around her coffee cup. Death would separate a mother and baby. What would happen to a baby with a dead mother?

Britt had worked with clients who'd lost their children due to drug addiction, and Child Protective Services had always stepped in to take charge of those kids until mom and dad got clean and sober.

She tapped her fingernail against her cup. Maybe she could start there. LA was a big city, but how many Russian mothers had given birth in the past two months?

She glanced at the time on her phone. Before she got back to the hotel to do some research on her laptop, she had a stop to make at the Tattle-Tale—or at least the alley behind the Tattle-Tale.

Did Calvin hang out there all day or just at

night? She'd seen him only at night, but then, she'd been at the Tattle-Tale only at night.

Alexei had already paid the bill and left the tip, so Britt scooted her chair back from the table and hiked up the street to her car. She drove to the club and parked around the corner.

Daylight didn't do much to improve the alley, although more businesses had their doors open, and the midday sun expelled the lurking shadows and hidden corners.

She strode down the middle of the asphalt, veering to the right as a car rolled past her. As she approached the back of the Tattle-Tale, she peered around the corner of the Dumpster where Calvin usually parked his basket.

He'd found another location today, or maybe he had a different hangout during the day.

The back door of the Tattle-Tale burst open and Britt jumped, her hand to her heart.

"Hey, Barbie. You come to see me?" Stepan grinned as he hoisted a plastic garbage bag into the Dumpster.

"N-no." *Damn, what timing.* "I was hoping someone would be here though. I wanted to check my time card. I think I forgot to clock out the other night."

He stepped back and shoved the door wider. "What luck."

She took a few tentative steps toward the open door, but Stepan didn't budge. Instead, he swept his arm forward, ushering her inside the building.

Stepan wasn't a big man, but he hadn't left her much room, so she had to squeeze past him, getting a whiff of stale coffee and cigarettes from his breath.

"How about that mess last night, eh?" He let the door slam behind them, and Britt jumped again—this time internally.

"That was pretty crazy. Do you know if there was even a fire?"

"Just sprinklers. Faulty system maybe, but all those fine people ruined their fine clothes."

His lips twisted into a sneer, and Britt thought about Alexei's comment about disgruntled employees—not that she'd trust Stepan here and now. If Alexei wanted to feel him out, she'd leave that up to him.

"What are you doing here so early?"

"Little cleaning, little inventory." His dull eyes narrowed as she made a beeline for the rack of time cards. "You can't check your time card tonight?"

"I'm off tonight." She flicked her time card

out of the rack and squinted at it. "Oh, good. I did clock out."

"Now that I have you here." He stepped into the hallway, blocking her access to the back door. "You want to help a little behind bar? Just polishing glasses. I'll tell Irina and you get some extra pay."

She opened her mouth as every fiber in her body screamed *No*, but then the memory of Jerome sneaking behind the bar that first night she'd met Alexei flashed into her brain. She'd never been able to get behind the bar since that night without arousing suspicions.

"You know, I could use a few extra bucks." She brushed her hands together. "What do you need?"

"The glasses get spots. Sergei don't like spots." He whipped a towel from his waistband and pressed it into her hands. "You go behind bar and check all shot glasses. Spots? You wipe clean."

"I can do that. Didn't have anything planned anyway."

"Pretty girl like you, no boyfriend? No hot date?"

Oh, I have a hot Russian boyfriend, but only in my mind.

"I just moved to this area. I don't know a lot of people."

He gave her a sidelong glance. "You knew Jerome."

She sucked in a breath and held the towel to her face. "Don't remind me. That was terrifying."

"Not a good date." He shook his head as if Jerome had planned to get murdered on their date.

"It wasn't a date, really. He knew I was new to town." She hunched her shoulders. "It was awful."

"You saw it happen?"

He'd shuffled closer, and she couldn't breathe. She'd been crazy to stay here with him.

"No." She took a few steps back. "I couldn't find parking. It was all over by the time I got out of my car and walked to Sunset. Not a great invitation to the city or to dating."

"Better luck next time."

She spun around and called over her shoulder. "I'll get going on those glasses. What are you going to be doing?"

"Checking inventory in supply room." He held up a clipboard.

Her pulse didn't steady until she was behind the bar and she could hear Stepan banging around in the back. Aware of the camera watching her every move, Britt parked in front of a plastic dish rack of shot glasses and plucked out the first one.

She held it up to the light over the bar and rubbed it with the cloth Stepan had given her. She and Alexei had reviewed the footage from that night, and Jerome had been able to avoid the camera by ducking behind the bar near the sink. She'd do the same. Whatever Jerome had done that night, it hadn't taken him long.

She worked her way through the rows of glasses in the first rack and then shuffled to the next one—one step closer to the sink. She finished that set and stationed herself in front of the third, right next to the sink and above the area where Jerome had been crouching that night.

With one row of glasses polished, Britt shook out the cloth and peered at it. She dropped it on the bar and squatted down on her haunches.

Stacks of cocktail napkins, pads of paper for orders, matchbooks and pencil stubs littered the shelves beneath the bar.

She hunched forward and reached past a stack of coasters. Her fingertips brushed cold hard metal. She traced an oblong box with her hands and pulled it off the shelf, knocking several coasters onto the floor.

She set the strong box on the floor and flicked up the latch with trembling fingers. She lifted the lid and stirred the contents with her index finger. Old receipts and a few pictures of women in various stages of undress rustled and shifted in the box.

Could these pictures be important? Had Jerome taken them? She picked up a few and shuffled through them.

A broken plastic band fell on the floor, and Britt picked it up. She smoothed out the slightly curled bracelet against her knee, and her heart jumped as she saw the name Tatyana printed on the plastic.

Britt leaned back to get the band in the light, and as she read the words printed there, her blood ran cold. In her hands, she held Tatyana Porizkova's hospital bracelet, dated about a month ago.

How had it gotten here? Was this hospital stay related to the birth of Tatyana's baby? She snatched one of the receipts from the box and scribbled down the information from the bracelet.

"How's it going?" Stepan called from the hallway.

Britt shoved the receipt and wristband into

her pocket and closed the lid on the metal box. She replaced it on the shelf, arranging the other items in front of it, and popped up from behind the bar just as Stepan rounded the corner.

"I'm almost done with this third set of shot glasses."

"Barbie, you're slow. Can you do that whole row?"

"Sure I can." She finished polishing the rest of the glasses with her mind racing. Jerome knew the bracelet was there but hadn't wanted to take it in case someone noticed it was missing. Either that or he found it and put it there himself. But he wouldn't have hidden something like that at the club. Was that what he'd planned on telling her the night he died? Was he going to tell her about Tatyana's baby and the significance of that baby?

She could understand why the Belkins wouldn't want one of their women to get pregnant, but why would they go to such great lengths to hide that pregnancy or even harm the pregnant woman and anyone who knew about the pregnancy? How could a little baby bring down a criminal organization like the Belkins'?

The caller had been right. She had to find

Tatyana's baby. That baby seemed to hold the key to everything.

She fingered the hospital band in the front pocket of her jeans. And now she knew exactly where to start—Cedars-Sinai Medical Center.

Stepan joined her behind the bar and elbowed her in the ribs. "You do good job, Barbie."

"Thanks." She laced her fingers together and stretched them in front of her. "I'm going to take off now. Are you going to Mila's party at Rage tonight?"

"In my dreams." He rolled his eyes to the ceiling. "Girls only, just dancers and waitresses. You going?"

"No, I'm going to get to bed early. Have a good night."

"Enjoy hot date, Barbie."

She snorted and slid out from behind the bar. Grabbing her purse from a chair, she waved.

Outside the club, she rested her back against the door and scooped in a deep breath of garbage-scented air. What was that bracelet doing there?

She pushed off the door and tripped as a man emerged from behind the Dumpster, her nerves still raw. Calvin had appeared after all.

As the raggedy man shuffled forward, her heart dipped. A different transient had taken Calvin's spot, a younger man.

"Sorry, I thought you were someone else." She held up her hands to the homeless man planted in front of her.

"You lookin' for Calvin?"

She glanced over her shoulder at the back door of the Tattle-Tale. "Well, sort of. Do you know where he is today?"

"He don't come here in daytime." The man tugged at the dirty cap on his head. "Do you wanna know where he crashes during the day?"

Britt eyed the rough hand thrust at her, palm up. She dug into her purse and pulled out a ten-dollar bill. She waved it at him. "Will this tell me?"

"Uh-huh."

She tucked the money into his hand, and it disappeared into the capacious folds of his coat, draped over his slouched form in the seventy-five-degree heat.

"He's in the park down on the corner." He jerked his thumb to the right.

"There's a park on this street?"

"That patch of grass and trees near the free-way on-ramp." He tapped his temple with one finger. "You know Calvin ain't quite right in the head."

"Are you saying he's dangerous?" Britt took a step back from the cloud of alcohol fumes emanating from the man's pores. This guy seemed a lot sketchier than Calvin.

"Nah, just don't know what business you'd have with him."

"Business? I wouldn't call it business." She pointed to the end of the alley. "That way and then left toward the freeway?"

"That's it. Can't miss it."

Britt heard a click behind her and spun around. She stared at the metal door leading to the club. "Was that door open?"

Her homeless guide hunched into his coat. "Nope."

"All right, then. Thanks for the tip."

She exited the alley on the other side and got into her car. She drove up the street to the so-called park with its scrappy patches of dried grass and bushes that dotted a trail to the area beneath the on-ramp.

She parked the car and gripped the steering wheel, puffing out short breaths as she watched a man duck under the canopy of trees by the on-ramp. Calling this a park was generous. It looked like there could be a homeless camp beneath the freeway, away from prying eyes.

Maybe if she just stood on the sidewalk and yelled for Calvin, he'd come out to meet her. She didn't think she wanted to see what inhabited this particular urban gathering place.

After debating the wisdom of visiting a homeless camp, Britt grabbed her cell phone from the cup holder and opened the car door. She could get 911 on speed dial if she had to.

Putting one foot in front of the other, she marched toward the edge of the sidewalk. She cupped her hand over her mouth to make her voice heard above the roar of the freeway. "Calvin? Calvin, are you in there?"

She held her breath, listening for an answer. Several seconds later, she stepped onto a patch of grass, rough with pebbles scattered through it. "Calvin? It's Barbie. I—I have something for you."

Britt jerked as something crashed through the bushes, and a man stumbled into the clearing from beneath the pillars of cement. Calvin, his jacket ripped and bloody, staggered toward her and keeled forward.

Her heart rattling her rib cage, Britt launched forward and dropped to the ground beside him. "Calvin? What happened?"

He sucked in a wet breath, and a line of

blood trickled from the corner of his mouth. Up close, she could see his battered face and split lip. She put her hands on his thin body to feel if he had any other injuries or if any blood was seeping through his clothing.

Calvin coughed and strangled out one word.

"What?" She put her ear close to his lips. "What did you say?"

He rasped, "Nothing. I know nothing about Lee-Low."

Britt caught her breath. Childlike, Calvin had just admitted he *did* know something about Leanna.

She whispered, "What don't you know about Lee-Low, Calvin? I won't tell anyone."

His cloudy eyes shifted over her shoulder and widened for a split second—right before a boot landed against her ribs.

Chapter Thirteen

Back from the warehouse and ensconced in the luxury of his hotel suite, Alexei tapped Send on his phone and blew out a breath. He'd just secured proof positive that the Belkin crime family had taken delivery of a shipment of weapons—none that they needed to run their little empire here in LA. These weapons could start a war or two, and as much as the Belkins destroyed any area they inhabited, they counted on the niceties of society to keep selling their drugs and women to any wealthy takers.

Those arms were meant for someone else, most likely in exchange for the raw opium Vlad could provide the Belkins from the fields of Afghanistan. Ariel had to see the sense in pursuing this connection—and had to see the sense in keeping him on the assignment. He'd already infiltrated the Belkins at the inner-most levels.

He watched his phone, but if he expected Ariel to respond immediately, it looked like he'd be disappointed.

His eyebrows shot up when he noticed the time on his cell. He'd been surprised that he'd made it back to the hotel before Britt. Wasn't she going to poke around the baby angle? She couldn't do that over the phone?

He'd declined to give her his cell phone number because he didn't want it in her cell phone contacts, but he should've bought a temp phone so she could contact him.

What he *had* done, without her knowledge, was install a tracking device on her cell phone, and after the attack on her last night, he felt justified. Now he felt worried.

He called up the locator on his phone and cursed in Russian when he saw the pin in Hollywood, right near the Tattle-Tale. Why had she gone to the club? She didn't even have a shift tonight.

His pulse picked up speed. Unless she didn't go to the club willingly. Who knew what that thug who'd had her around the throat told his bosses?

He swept the keys to his bike from the TV stand and rushed downstairs. He secured his phone on the handlebars of the motorcycle so he could watch the locator app.

When he rolled past the entrance to the Tattle-Tale, still closed, he drew his brows over his nose. The pin on the app had shifted, no longer located at the Tattle-Tale but still in the area.

He gunned his bike and made a U-turn, following the GPS on the phone. When he saw Britt's car parked on the street near the freeway on-ramp, he swallowed hard. Had she broken down in that old rattletrap she drove?

As he rolled up behind the empty car, an icy fear dragged a finger down his back. Where had she gone?

He parked his bike on the street and pulled his helmet off his head. The muffled cries he heard had him sprinting toward the noises coming from the area below the on-ramp.

He couldn't see anything until he got to the sidewalk that bordered the grassy strip. And then what he saw fueled a burning rage in his gut, and he flew at the man pummeling Britt, who was flailing her arms at her attacker and bicycling her legs from her position on the ground.

Alexei tackled the man, gagging on the sour stench rising from his body. Alexei slammed his fist into the man's face and had the satis-faction of hearing a distinct crack.

Blood poured from the guy's nose, and he spit out a stream of foul expletives as he swung at Alexei. Alexei stepped back from the punch and then kneed the man in the gut, bringing him to the ground.

Britt tugged on his sleeve. "Let's go. I don't want to be here when the cops arrive. I just called 911. Calvin's hurt."

"Calvin?" Alexei stomped on the man's hand, the same hand he'd been using to beat Britt. He crushed it beneath his boot until the man screamed in agony.

Alexei looked up to see Britt crouched beside another homeless man, his face bloody and broken.

She whispered something to Calvin and then launched herself at Alexei. "Please, we need to get out of here to avoid questions."

The sound of a siren in the distance up-rooted Alexei's feet from the ground. "Meet me at the diner where we went the first night we met."

Britt nodded and jogged to her car.

Alexei followed her the three blocks to the diner. She parked first and sat in the car. When he got off his bike, he approached the driver's-side window, which she powered down.

"Do you want to tell me what just happened back there?"

"How did you find me?"

"We'll discuss this inside. You need some ice for your eye. Head to the restroom as soon as you get inside to clean up." He reached inside the car and flicked some weed stems from her hair. "Are you all right?"

She dabbed her fingertips across her face and gazed at the smears of blood on her fingers. "I'm okay."

They entered the diner, and Alexei grabbed a table in the back, next to a window on the parking lot, while Britt scurried to the restroom, head down, hair creating a veil on either side of her face.

He asked for a couple of waters and kept one eye on the plastic menu and the other on the parking lot. He didn't know what to expect right now. Why had two homeless men been fighting with Britt?

She emerged from the bathroom with a puffy bottom lip and a red mark at the corner of her eye, but she'd cleaned up the blood and looked better than he'd expected.

She slid into the booth across from him and sucked down half the water with a straw. Then she closed her eyes and rested the back of her head against the red vinyl banquette.

"Do you want to start at the beginning?"

She opened an eye—the one not rimmed in red. "How'd you find me?"

"I put a tracker on your phone, but that's not important. Tell me what happened."

"I went to the Tattle-Tale to find Calvin to see if he could tell me any more about Leanna. I didn't expect anyone to be there."

"Who was there?"

"Stepan the bartender."

"That's just great. What story did you tell him for being there?"

"I told him I wanted to check my time card. He believed me."

"As far as you know."

"I really don't think Stepan is involved too much in the criminal activities."

"Did you check it and leave?" Alexei looked up and smiled at the waitress. "I'll have a cup of coffee and a piece of lemon meringue pie."

"I'll have a diet soda, whatever you have, and the grilled cheese sandwich." She shrugged at Alexei. "I missed lunch."

When the waitress took their menus and left, Alexei stuck his fingers in his water, fished out a couple of ice cubes and wrapped them in a napkin. "Put this on your right eye, and maybe you can avoid a shiner."

Britt pressed the makeshift ice pack to her

face. "I was at the club for more than a few minutes. Stepan corralled me into helping him."

"You stayed there with him? Alone?"

"He was okay after a few of his clumsy attempts at flirtation. I think he just does it because it's expected. He really doesn't try that hard."

"Go on." Alexei circled his finger in the air. "How did you get from helping Stepan in the Tattle-Tale to being some transient's punching bag?"

"Remember that first night when we saw Jerome return to the club and duck behind the bar, out of the camera's eye?"

He'd never forget that night when he'd met Britt. "Yeah, of course I remember."

"I thought it would be a good opportunity for me to get down there and see what was so important. I haven't been able to get behind the bar yet during one of my shifts." Her knees, bouncing beneath the table, knocked his. She must've found something, and she was dying to tell him.

"And?" He hunched forward.

She rose up slightly from her seat and pulled something from her pocket. She tossed it on the table between them.

He ran the pad of his thumb over the curled-up piece of plastic, reading the words printed there. "It's Tatyana's hospital bracelet from Cedars-Sinai. So, she had that mystery baby in the hospital. You found this beneath the bar?"

"It was in one of those metal lock boxes, but it wasn't even locked. It was just in there with other junk, but Jerome must've known it was there. Maybe he found it at the club, but what would it be doing there?"

"I doubt Jerome found it." Alexei scuffed his knuckles against the stubble on his chin. "He wouldn't keep it at the club. He might've discovered it in that box. He wouldn't want to take it to tip anyone off, so maybe he went back to take a picture of it."

Britt bounced in her seat. "I never thought of that. Of course, he took a picture. During the staged mugging, his attacker stole his phone. But that doesn't explain why the wristband was there in the first place."

"I think it's obvious." Alexei steepled his fingers and peered at Britt over the tips. "Tatyana must've been at the Tattle-Tale wearing her hospital ID."

She crossed her arms, hugging her body. "Why would they have her there after she'd just given birth? What did they do with her?"

"I don't know, but now we know where that baby was born."

"I hope…" She pressed her fingertips against her lips. "I mean, they wouldn't kill a baby, would they?"

"Your female caller told you to find the baby. It sounds like she knew what she was talking about, and she wouldn't have you looking for a dead baby, would she?" He grabbed Britt's hand and chafed it between his. "Finding that bracelet was great, but that doesn't explain the attack on Calvin and you."

Britt paused as the waitress delivered their food.

As she cut her sandwich in half, she said, "I finished up my work with Stepan and left out the back. I saw a transient, and I thought he was Calvin at first and said his name. He wasn't Calvin but said he'd tell me where he was—for a price. So I handed him a ten, and he directed me to that area by the on-ramp."

Alexei rolled his eyes. "You thought it was a good idea to pay a homeless man for information and then head to an obvious homeless camp under the freeway?"

She brushed her fingertips together, sending a shower of crumbs onto her plate. "I was going to stand away from those bushes and call Calvin out to me."

"Didn't work out that way, huh?"

"Calvin did come out of the bushes, beaten and bloodied, and fell to the ground. I went to him, and out of the blue he said he didn't know anything about Lee-Low." She took a big bite of her sandwich, and after she swallowed she dabbed a napkin against her mouth. "Which of course means he *does* know something about her."

"Maybe, maybe not. He knew that's what you were going to ask him about. Maybe he had a moment of clarity and was telling you the truth. He knew Lee-Low from the club, she was nice to him, you were nice to him and you reminded him of Lee-Low." Alexei flicked a dab of meringue from his pie and sucked it off his finger. "How'd the other guy get involved?"

"While I was trying to help Calvin, the other guy attacked me. Kicked me in the gut for starters."

"Was he with Calvin? Did he try to rob you?"

She dropped her sandwich on her plate. "The Belkins sent him, Alexei. He was the same guy I had talked to in the alley."

The dread that had been building in his gut reached up and grabbed him by the throat.

He'd suspected Britt's run-in with the transient had something to do with the club, but he'd been hoping it was random. No such luck.

He shoved his plate away, the tart lemon now sour on his tongue. "How did they arrange that? The Belkins must've paid the other transient to beat up Calvin, or they had one of their henchmen do it, and then they had him lure you to that spot by the freeway."

"That's what I thought as soon as I realized who was attacking me."

"It was Stepan."

"Wait. What? How do you figure? Irina was the one who saw me with Calvin."

"But Stepan is the only one who saw you today. When you got there, he probably called Irina or Sergei and put out the word. They beat up Calvin as a warning and ordered the other transient to attack you. Do you think Calvin's going to make it?"

"I think so. I didn't see any mortal wounds, and he was talking to me. The beating I took, while not—" she dabbed her fingers high on her cheekbone beneath her eye "—pleasant, wasn't life-threatening either. What was the reason behind that?"

"It was a warning. They have no idea what you know or why you're talking to Calvin. They do know Calvin hangs out behind the Tattle-Tale. He may have seen things, even if he doesn't understand what those things mean. They don't want you or anyone else talking to Calvin and getting any ideas. Of course..." He smooshed a piece of piecrust with the tines of his fork.

"Of course what?"

He flicked Tatyana's hospital band with his finger. "You did take this."

"I wasn't thinking. I had it in my hand, and Stepan was coming. Maybe I should put it back."

"Not now."

"Maybe they won't be looking for it. It seems like someone tossed it in that box as an afterthought. Jerome just ran across it because that's his domain. They wouldn't think it would mean anything to anybody."

"And yet it *did* mean something to Jerome—and it got him killed."

Britt licked her lips and took a gulp of her soda. "We don't know that. Due to your mad video skills, Sergei never saw Jerome return to the club that night and crouch below the bar."

"They could've seen him before. Maybe that's not the first time he looked at that wristband. Are you working tomorrow night?"

"Yes."

"I don't think it's a good idea for you to go in."

"I could put the bracelet back."

He shook his head. "An even worse idea."

"What about you?" She slumped in her seat and ripped a piece of crust from her sandwich. "Any luck?"

"As a matter of fact." He held up his index finger. "Wait—I haven't checked my messages."

"You communicated with Ariel? You found something?"

As he pulled his phone from his pocket, he said, "My new friend introduced me to a cache of weapons he has on the market, but only in limited quantities because he already has a big order."

"The Belkins?"

He glanced down at his phone and smacked the table. "Yes!"

"You have the okay from Ariel?"

He huddled closer to Britt over the table and read from the text. "'Sounds promising. Proceed.'"

"That's it?"

"There's an attachment with more info. I'll read it when we get back to the hotel." That knot he'd had between his shoulder blades melted away, and he took a big bite of pie.

"That's great, Alexei. You're official now."

"That'll mean a lot when it comes to resources. I'll have the whole CIA and FBI behind me now—or at least the parts that Ariel can tap into."

"I gather the Vlad task force itself is pretty hush-hush within these agencies?"

"Need to know, which is why you know just about everything. You're in this up to your neck." He picked up Tatyana's wristband by one jagged edge. "We're going to start using my newfound legitimacy with this."

"How?"

"We have hackers who can search a hospital's database. We're going to find out exactly why Tatyana was in the hospital, when and what happened to her baby."

"If my informant was right, finding the baby could cause havoc for the Belkins, and then they won't be in any position to negotiate with Vlad or anyone else."

Alexei drummed his fingers on the table. "I don't know how one baby could impact the Belkin crime family. If the baby belongs to some john, I don't know how we prove that, and even if we do, hookers and escorts have babies every day. It's not going to hurt the Belkins."

"I don't know. Maybe my source will call back. Maybe she works at the Tattle-Tale. That's why I have to keep going back there."

Britt picked up her phone from the table. "I'm going to call the hospital to see if I can find out anything about Calvin. Which one do you think he's at?"

"Cedars-Sinai—same hospital as Tatyana."

Britt widened her eyes. "That's perfect. I think we need to pay Calvin a visit."

"Are you up for that?" He shoved the pie plate at her. "At lcast finish my pie. You deserve pie for getting kicked in the ribs."

She wolfed down the last three bites and ended up with meringue on her chin.

He dabbed his finger on her face and sucked the sweetness into his mouth. "I'm gonna put that down to you not being able to feel your face after getting punched."

She smiled and grabbed his hand. "I'm glad you're legit now, Russki…and not just because of the perks."

"I am, too, but it doesn't mean I'm not taking Olav Belkin down—for good."

"I know that." She squeezed his hand. "But now it's sanctioned."

Sanctioned or not, Belkin was a dead man, but the fire that had roared in his chest every time he thought about Belkin had died down to a kindling. He still wanted to avenge his father's murder at Belkin's hands, but over the past week his passion had burned for a different cause—keeping this woman safe from harm.

As ALEXEI DROVE her car to the hospital, Britt's jaw ached, and she had one arm wrapped around her midsection, pressing against her sore ribs. Maybe she should be checking in herself.

If Alexei hadn't found her, how far would that homeless guy have gone? What marching orders had Sergei or Irina given him?

The strikes against her had been piling up. The Belkins knew she'd been in the vicinity when they'd murdered Jerome. Someone had seen her in that hallway where she witnessed Jessie, drugged and compromised. Irina had caught her talking to Calvin, and now she and Calvin had both paid in blood for that conversation.

What next? Would they finger her as the person who'd taken Tatyana's hospital wristband? Did Sergei even know the wristband was in that metal box? It seemed like a foolish place to hide evidence that could destroy an entire criminal operation.

Or maybe that phone call from the Russian woman had been a hoax just to play her.

She slid a glance at Alexei, hunched over the steering wheel to maneuver through LA traffic. Had he thought of that already? Probably. He didn't miss much, including her insane attraction to him.

Now she had to make good on her promise that she could have a fling with him and then let him go. The sigh escaped her lips before she could stop it.

"I know. Traffic is bad, but we're almost there."

"Emergency room, right?"

"We'll start there."

After parking the car on the rooftop of the parking structure, they made their way into the crowded emergency room and walked to the reception desk.

Britt folded her hands on the counter. "Excuse me. I saw…two men at the corner of Gower and the 101 off-ramp badly beaten and unconscious. I called 911 from my car but couldn't stop. I was wondering if they were okay. Can you tell me anything?"

The nurse at the desk didn't look up from her computer. "Are you a relative?"

"No, just a concerned citizen."

The nurse lifted one shoulder in a half-hearted attempt at sympathy. "We can't give out any information on patients. You can try calling the police. That would be LAPD's Hollywood Division."

Britt bit her bottom lip. "Can you at least tell me what floor Maternity is on?"

That got her attention. The nurse glanced up. "Ninth."

"Thanks."

Alexei put his hand on the small of her back and steered her out of the waiting room. When they reached the hallway, he stabbed the elevator button with his knuckle. "That was a waste of time."

She huffed out a breath as she stepped into the elevator car. "Try to do a good deed."

"Do you expect to have any better luck up there?" He jabbed his thumbs upward. "If anything, Maternity is going to be even more cautious."

"I just want to look around as long as we're here."

"I can get the info on Tatyana faster through my sources."

"We drove, we parked, we failed. Now we're here, so let's have a look."

Alexei saluted. "Right, chief."

"I like that other name better."

The elevator bumped and then settled on the ninth floor. They stepped out of the car, and the cheerful vibe lifted Britt's spirits. She bumped Alexei's shoulder with her own. "This sure beats the emergency room."

"Babies." He pointed down the hallway to a glassed-in room.

Britt approached the window and placed both hands on the glass. "Just look at them all. Getting ready to face the world."

"Everything ahead of them."

Britt began dragging her finger across the smooth pane of glass. "Rodriguez, Miller, Schwartz, Gomez, Rousseau."

Not all the babies were currently occupying their bassinets. Must be with their moms. She continued reading the names on the labels until she stumbled across a familiar one. She grabbed Alexei's arm. "The baby. Tatyana's baby."

"Where?" His body stiffened beside her.

"In the back row." She tapped on the window. "It's empty, but it says Baby Porizkova."

"You're kidding."

"I'm not. Do you see it? The label is pink. She had a girl."

"Could Tatyana still be here?" Alexei glanced over his shoulder, as if expecting to see her in the hallway behind them.

"I don't know. Do you think Jerome was wrong about her death? We can't very well poke our heads into all these rooms."

A nurse with a clipboard under her arm

came up to the nursery door and entered a code on the keypad.

"Excuse me?"

Alexei had nudged her in the back, but it was too late. The nurse turned at the door. "Yes?"

The nudge turned to a pinch, but Britt carried on anyway. "Where is the Porizkova baby?"

The nurse's eyes grew big, and Britt's stomach sank. At least Alexei had stopped jabbing her.

"Are you a relative?"

There it was again, that magical hospital word that opened doors and got you private information. Alexei spoke Russian. Maybe he could pose as a relative.

She took a breath, and Alexei's knuckle drove into her back, just below her sore ribs. He must've read her mind.

"N-no, but the name is familiar. My sister has a Russian friend, and I thought it might be the same person."

As wide as the nurse's eyes were a minute ago, she'd turned them into slits. "Was this friend pregnant?"

Alexei stepped beside her, his body vibrating with tension. "No. She wasn't pregnant. I don't even think that's the same name. You know those Russian names—always sound the same."

The nurse cocked her head. "What are you doing here?"

"We went to check on a friend in Emergency, and I thought it would be fun to look at the newborns." Britt giggled and patted her aching belly. "The old biological clock is ticking, I guess."

The nurse cracked a tight smile. "I'm sure you understand why we don't want strangers wandering around the nursery."

"Of course."

Alexei took Britt's arm. "Let's go see if Bob is ready to go yet."

He marched her down the hallway to the elevator with an iron grip on her wrist, as if he were afraid she'd run back to the nursery.

They stood shoulder to shoulder at the elevator, but Britt didn't dare say a word.

An older woman joined them, a canvas bag over her shoulder. "So sad for that little one."

Britt's gaze took in the woman head to toe. Not a nurse. She had a volunteer badge pinned to her sweater.

Britt gave her an encouraging smile, the kind she used to get her clients to divulge their deepest, darkest secrets. "The little Porizkova baby?"

"Yes. I heard you asking about her." She shook her gray curls. "Poor little mite doesn't have a mother."

"D-did her mother die in childbirth?"

"Worse." The volunteer pursed her lips.

What could be worse than death? Britt gave Alexei a quick glance. "What happened to her?"

"She up and walked out of the hospital after her little girl was born. Didn't say a word to anyone. Just up and disappeared."

"Oh." Britt put a hand to her thundering heart. "That's terrible. Maybe she didn't have a choice. At least she didn't abandon the baby later."

The woman sniffed. "Could've gone through the regular channels for adoption."

"Her baby's still here?"

"She was a preemie." The woman patted her bag. "I ought to know. I knit a cap for her. I knit all sizes, and that little one took the smallest size. I also cuddle the newborns, and that one's a sweetie."

Britt noticed Alexei wasn't poking her in the back during *this* conversation. "How long has the baby been here?"

The elevator doors opened, and Alexei held them open for the old woman.

"About a month. She's almost ready to leave, but where will she go without a mother?"

"I'm sure she'll be adopted by a loving family."

The woman spent the rest of the elevator ride talking about her knitting and the other newborns. When they parted ways in the parking structure, Britt turned to Alexei.

"What do you think happened?"

He put a finger to his lips. "Wait until we get to the car."

When they reached the nearly empty top level of the structure, Britt finally took a breath. They walked to the car, and Alexei opened the door for her. She slid inside, her knees bouncing as she waited for him to come around the other side.

When he shut the door, she rounded on him. "We did it. We found Tatyana's baby."

He ran his hands over the steering wheel but didn't start the car. "I don't think she left that baby on her own."

"Do you think the Belkins took her out of the hospital?"

"I'm sure of it. They probably would've taken the baby, too, if they could've made it past the dragon nurses."

Britt shivered. "Thank God for the dragon

nurses. Do you think they've tried to take the baby?"

"Maybe that's why the nurse went on high alert when you expressed interest in the Porizkova baby. That or she was going to call the police to question you." He smoothed a hand down her thigh. "Sorry for poking at you. That's what I was trying to avoid—questioning by the police."

"Yeah, that would've been a disaster." She yanked at her seat belt. "I think my sister knew something about this baby. Like you said before, if it were the trafficking and escort business, the Belkins could've gotten around that. There's something about that baby. Could the baby be addicted to drugs? Would the Belkins worry about that?"

Alexei's nostrils flared and his eyebrows collided over his nose. He yanked the keys from the ignition.

"Britt, get out of the car!"

"What?" Already on edge, she'd grabbed the handle.

"Out of the car! It's gonna blow."

The force of his voice pumped a flood of adrenaline into her system, and she pushed against the door. It swung open. She tumbled out.

Alexei was still shouting, so she sprinted

away from the car and waved at two people heading her way. She panted, "Stay back."

She didn't even hear her second word above the deafening explosion behind her. As the blast propelled her several feet forward and she hit the cement, she had just one thought. *Alexei.*

Chapter Fourteen

Britt's ears were ringing, but she could still hear the woman several feet away screaming. She raised her head, propping her chin on the cement floor of the parking structure, her head swimming. The two people who'd been walking toward her were still on their feet, but their white faces were a study in shock.

Groaning, Britt rolled over, her sore ribs making it hard to breathe—or maybe that was the acrid black smoke drifting toward her. Had Alexei made it out alive?

As she blinked her eyes, Alexei's face floated above her, and she sobbed out his name.

"Britt!" He dropped beside her. "Are you all right?"

She sat up, clutching her midsection. "I am now. Was anyone hurt?"

"There weren't that many cars up on this

level. Nobody on my side." He tipped his head toward the two people by the elevator, hugging. "They got lucky. You saved their lives."

"You saved my life." She held up her purse, still hanging over her shoulder. "I'll call 911."

"Let them do it. Let's get out of here."

"My car."

"Destroyed. You don't want to explain to the police why the car of a waitress at the Tattle-Tale was sabotaged. We don't want the police nosing around and revealing your true identity…or mine, until we can get what we need from the Belkins."

"Won't the police track the car to me anyway? Or at least to Barbie Jones?"

"Not if I, or the task force, have anything to say about it." He wrapped his arms around her gently. "Can you stand up?"

"Yes." She leaned on Alexci, and he rose to his feet, pulling her up with him. Her legs wobbled like cooked spaghetti, but she grabbed his arm and the world steadied.

As they passed the couple, still clinging to each other, Alexei held up his phone. "You okay? We're going to call 911."

They both nodded, still in shock.

They weren't the only ones. Britt hung on to Alexei as he bypassed the elevator. On their way down the stairs, they met a few people rushing up to the rooftop parking level.

One man asked them, "What happened?"

"Some couple's car exploded. They're okay though. Nobody hurt." He brushed past the man, towing Britt along with him.

When they reached the street level, Britt finally felt like she could breathe, and she scooped in a big breath even though her ribs protested.

She grabbed Alexei's hands. "Do I look as messed up as you do?"

"Just a little smudged. Do I look like I've been through hell?" The sirens wailing down the street propelled Alexei into motion again. "Let's keep walking."

Britt tripped and looked down at her sandal. "My sandal's broken."

Alexei glanced up and down the street. "Let's go to that fast-food restaurant and clean up in the bathroom before we go back to the hotel."

By the time Britt washed the soot and dirt from her face, arms and legs, ran her hands through her tangled, smoky hair and returned to the restaurant, Alexei was seated at a plastic table with two drinks in front of him.

He looked up from his phone, where he was texting. "I got you a diet soda, but it's self-serve, so you can dump that and get what you want."

"This is fine." She collapsed into the hard chair across from him and sucked down the soda, the cold drink soothing to her scratchy throat. She tipped her drink toward his phone, as he placed it on the table. "Texting Ariel?"

"Yeah. That's the downside to being official—I have to report everything, especially if I want the task force to take action."

"Like covering up the owner of an exploding car?"

"Exactly."

Britt toyed with her straw, almost afraid to ask the next logical question. She cleared her throat. "How'd they know I was at the hospital?"

"We weren't followed. I know that for a fact. I kept watch and took a few evasive moves on our way from the diner to the hospital. There's no way someone followed us."

"That means…?"

"It means they put a tracker on your car."

She squeezed her cup so hard, she popped the lid. "When and why did they do that?"

"You're kidding, right? The Belkins have several reasons to suspect you—your so-called date with Jerome the night they offed him, your presence outside the room where they were holding a drugged waitress and your conversations with a transient who probably knows more about the Tattle-Tale than he realizes. When you showed up at the club and you didn't even have a shift, they figured enough was enough."

"Do you think Stepan told Sergei I was there, and they put the bug on my car then?"

"Probably. I hope so."

"Really?" She shook the ice in her cup. "Why is that?"

"Because if they put the tracker on your car last night during the party, they know you went to a hotel in Beverly Hills instead of back to your hovel in Hollywood."

"As it is, they know I left the club, stopped by the homeless hangout under the freeway, went to a diner down the street and then went to the hospital. That's not incriminating."

"The same hospital where Tatyana's baby is currently taking up a bassinet in the nursery?"

"The same hospital where the ambulance took Calvin after his beating. Wouldn't it make sense I'd check up on him?"

"Maybe." Alexei shrugged and winced. "Until they realize Tatyana's hospital band is missing. They just tried to kill you, Britt. I don't think Belkin is buying that you were at

Cedars-Sinai to check on Calvin—or at least he's not taking any chances."

Britt propped her forehead in her hand, and one tear leaked from the corner of her eye. "If they tried to kill me for my suspicious behavior, they must've killed Leanna—only she didn't have a navy SEAL protecting her. As usual, I lead the charmed life, and she gets the short end of the stick."

The tear rolled down her cheek and trembled on the edge of her jaw until Alexei dabbed at it with his rough fingertip. He whispered, "I would've helped Leanna if I could have, too."

Tilting her head, she rested her cheek in the palm of his hand. "I know you would have, but you were here for me, not her."

"I'm sorry I wasn't here for Leanna, but I thank God I was here for you." He traced the shell of her ear. "Let's get back to the hotel so I can put some queries into motion—we're going to find out everything we can about Tatyana and the birth of that baby."

When they got back to the hotel, Britt collapsed on the sofa and closed her eyes. "I suppose this means I can't return to work at the Tattle-Tale."

The cushion next to hers sank as Alexei sat next to her, and her body tilted toward his, her shoulder bumping his. He felt solid, and she didn't move, resting against him.

"Now that they've determined you're public enemy number one, they could do anything to you there—drug you, arrange for an accident, kidnap you. No, you're not going back." He held out his phone, cupped in his hand. "My sources are already expunging your name from that car, and Ariel has someone hacking the records at Cedars-Sinai to get information on Tatyana and her baby, although that's not where she wants my focus."

Britt opened one eye and rolled her head to the side. "She wants you back on the arms dealer."

"That's what's going to bring down Belkin." He kissed the top of her head. "You must be starving. It's late for dinner."

"My stomach is still in knots. I don't know if I could eat anything."

"You managed to wolf down a grilled cheese sandwich after that transient kicked the stuffing out of you."

"Yeah, then things escalated a hundredfold from getting punched a few times to getting my car blown up." Her cell phone buzzed from her purse on the floor, and she leaned over to grab it.

Alexei put his hand on her arm and asked, "Who is it?"

"It's—" she peered at the display and bolted upright "—it's that number from before—the woman who told me about Tatyana's baby. Maybe she knows we were at the hospital."

Before he could stop her, she answered the call and put it on speaker for Alexei to hear. "Hello?"

"Don't hello me, you Russian whore."

Britt jerked her head to the side to stare at Alexei, whose mouth had dropped open.

"Excuse me?" She tried to put on her best Russian accent.

"I've been trying to catch my husband, Gary, for months now, and I finally found your number on his phone."

"Gary?"

"Don't play dumb. I know he's been sneaking around behind my back to see you. I even know your name—*Mila*."

Britt covered her mouth with her hand. "I—I…"

"You'd better find some other sugar daddy. I'm warning you. Stay away from my husband."

The outraged wife ended the call, and Britt dropped the phone. "It was Mila. She called me from her boyfriend's phone to tell me about Tatyana's baby."

"We can't be absolutely sure it was Mila. It could've been any of the women. Maybe this Gary was at a party with several of the dancers from the club. It could've been any one of them."

"Maybe, but there's one sure way to find out."

"How are you going to get in touch with Mila? You're not going back to the club."

"I know she's working tonight. It's her last night, and the other women are having a party for her at Rage."

"Rage? Why would they pick that place?"

"I don't know, but I plan to be there."

"Absolutely not. What if the Belkins are there?"

"The Belkins aren't going to be there. This is for the women only. Stepan told me."

"You asked Stepan about the party?" He drove two fingers against his temple and massaged.

"I just wanted to confirm it was Mila's last night. Why would he be suspicious about that? I told him I wasn't going."

"Sergei is obviously suspicious about everything you say and do, and Stepan seems to be a loyal lackey."

"I'm going, and… I want you there, too."

"Nothing could keep me away." He cupped her face in his hands, and his blue eyes blazed in the same way they did when he talked about avenging his father's death.

An answering flame leaped in her heart along with the hope that this time that passion burned for her.

BRITT'S TAXI PULLED up in front of the Rage nightclub at two thirty in the morning, and she didn't even look at the spot where Jerome had been felled. Instead, she straightened her tight skirt and strutted to the door.

After 2:00 a.m., Rage turned into a private club, but that just meant an increase in the cover charge and a more exclusive clientele as the club turned away potential patrons. The bouncer didn't turn her away, and Britt sashayed into the dark, crowded room.

High-pitched giggling led her to the corner where the women from the Tattle-Tale clustered around two or three sofas and several bottles of expensive champagne.

Britt waved to a few of the women and tried to catch Mila's eye, but the dancer didn't even look up when Britt joined the group. Maybe Alexei had been right and some other woman had called her from Gary's phone.

Theanessa bumped Britt's arm. "You didn't work tonight, Barbie?"

"I had the night off, but I didn't want to miss the party."

Mila's gaze shifted to Britt over the edge of her champagne glass and bounced away as quickly.

Britt grabbed a flute of the bubbly from the table and downed half of it. The warmth of the booze immediately seeped into her muscles.

Several men approached their group and pulled some of the women onto the dance floor. Shaking off an invitation from one of them, Britt scanned the crowd for Alexei. She thought she saw him a couple of times, but couldn't be sure.

Would any of the women from the Tattle-Tale recognize him?

The spot on the sofa next to Mila finally cleared, and Britt parked next to her. "How was your last night?"

Mila tossed back her champagne and grabbed another glass. "Like every other night."

"You're going to work for the Belkins in… another capacity?"

Mila's fingers tightened on the delicate stem of the glass. "What are you doing here, Barbie? You should go home."

Britt took a long, shaky breath. "I spoke to your lover's wife tonight."

The glass jerked in Mila's hand and the golden liquid sloshed over the edge. Mila licked her fingers. "My lover?"

"Gary. The man whose phone you used to call me." Britt pinned her gaze on Mila and didn't move a muscle. Had she gone too far?

"I've told you all I'm going to tell you... Britt."

"I need more. There's someone who can help us, help Tatyana."

"Tatyana dead."

Britt gulped. "Help her baby, then. Her baby is still at the hospital. The Belkins already know I was there. They planted an explosive device on my car."

"Baby in danger." Mila's hands were shaking too much to hold the glass. "You have police? Someone to help?"

"Yes."

The dancer's wide eyes darted around the club. "Not here. They watch." She tapped her arm near the tattoo. "They follow with tracker."

"The ladies' room?" Britt grabbed Mila's hand. "Come with me."

They ducked into the back hallway with three single-use bathrooms and found one empty. Once inside, Britt locked the door behind them.

"Tell me what you know about Tatyana's baby, about my sister."

Mila rotated her arm at the elbow to display her tattoo with a red mark next to it. "Your sister like me—tattooed for Belkins and tracker implanted under skin. Ready for trafficking."

Britt sagged against the wall. "Where? Where is she? Where's Jessie?"

"Warehouse in Van Nuys."

"And the baby? What's so important about Tatyana's baby that the Belkins would kill to keep quiet?"

"The baby is old man's—Olav Belkin. Old *Vory v Zakone.*" Mila ran a finger across her throat. "Very bad. Very dangerous."

Britt's stomach churned. "I still don't understand. We both know the Belkins can work their way out of that."

"Not this time. Tatyana seventeen. Tatyana only seventeen." Mila grabbed Britt's hands. "Do you understand? This underage, no agreeing—it bring Belkin down. Do you understand?"

"Even if the sex is consensual, it's not legal."

"Yes, not consensual. They take baby tonight. They kill baby. They destroy the evidence."

"No! We won't let them hurt that baby. They won't hurt any more people."

A zinging noise came from outside the bathroom, and the hair on the back of Britt's neck stood up as she twisted toward the door.

Two seconds later, the door exploded inward as someone put his boot through it. In another second, the barrel of a gun followed, and Mila's body jerked.

Mila's hand clenched Britt's for a moment until another shot hit her in the chest and she dropped to the floor.

Chapter Fifteen

Alexei's pulse picked up speed when he saw Britt and the Ukrainian dancer slip into the back of the club. His pulse went into overdrive when he saw the goon at the bar push away from his beer and lumber after them.

Shoving his hand into the inside pocket of his jacket and closing his fingers around the grip of his gun, Alexei followed them. If he'd gotten his gun into this club, that other guy probably hadn't had any difficulty either.

Alexei sidled around the corner to the dark hallway, dotted with a few restrooms and leading to the back alley. The man turned once, and Alexei dived behind a machine dispensing condoms.

As he straightened up, Alexei heard the crash of splintering wood and the distinct whizzing sound of a silencer. The blood roared in his ears as he raced down the hall-way, his weapon raised and ready.

When he reached the open door, the scene before him clicked as if in a single picture—Mila dead on the floor, Britt hovering above her, the man's gun tracking toward the back of Britt's head.

Alexei squeezed the trigger, and the man keeled over—on top of Britt in the small space.

He took a step inside the bathroom and cranked his head over his shoulder at a woman coming their way. "Not this one. Someone's really sick in here."

"Ugh." She made a U-turn and disappeared inside another restroom.

By the time he turned around, Britt had wriggled from beneath the dead man. "We have to leave—now."

"No kidding." Alexei stepped over the shooter and grabbed Britt's arm, pulling her up. "Back door."

She squeezed past him into the hallway, and Alexei shoved the man's body farther into the bathroom, locked the door from the inside and slammed it.

When they hit the alleyway, Britt grabbed his jacket. "We have to go to the hospital and get the baby. Belkin's going to kill her tonight."

Alexei called up a car on his phone while he took Britt by the hand and hustled her out of the alley. "What did Mila tell you?"

"The baby is Olav Belkin's—and Tatyana was only seventeen. It's statutory rape, and the DNA from the baby can prove it."

Alexei didn't think his fury at Belkin could get any more heated—but he was wrong. "That bastard. He's gonna pay—for everything."

The car Alexei had called up from an online service pulled up to the curb several doors down from Rage and flashed its lights.

Alexei crowded Britt into the back seat and told the driver to take them to Cedars-Sinai. "And hurry."

The driver joked, "She's not pregnant, is she?"

Britt hunched forward in her seat. "No, but this is about a baby, so step on it."

In a low voice, Britt told Alexei the rest of Mila's story about the warehouse of women waiting to be groomed and trafficked. Alexei knew this story—if the women weren't already addicted to drugs, they would be by the time they left that warehouse.

He hoped to God Britt's sister was still alive by the time the place was raided. If they could get their hands on that baby, Belkin's associates and maybe even his own son would be singing like canaries…and Vlad wouldn't be able to do business with the Belkins under so much scrutiny.

Dragging his phone from his pocket, Alexei whispered to Britt. "I'm contacting Ariel now. She'll make it easy to get protection for that baby."

"Can she do it now? Mila seemed to think the Belkins were coming for the baby tonight."

"We'll be there until Ariel can get reinforcements. We'll protect that little baby."

The driver squealed to a stop in front of the hospital. "Record time."

"Thanks." Alexei waved his phone. "I'll add a big tip for you."

With his hand on Britt's back, Alexei hustled them both into the quiet lobby of the hospital. They took the elevator up to the maternity floor, but as soon as they stepped out of the car, his senses went on high alert.

The hallway and front desk were completely dark, and the nurses were murmuring among themselves.

One of them called out from the darkness. "Get Maintenance to get our backup generator going and do a check on all the patients."

"It's go time." Alexei squeezed Britt's shoulder. "They're here."

Her body jerked. "The baby."

Somebody screamed at the other end of the hallway, and Alexei tensed his muscles. "Maybe they already took her. Wait here."

Alexei spun around, following the noises through the hallway, glowing with auxiliary lights. A group of people were crowded around something on the floor, and Alexei's gut lurched.

He shouldered his way through and let out a puff of air when he saw an orderly slumped on the floor, groaning.

"What happened?"

A nurse turned her pale face toward him, her eyes dark and wide. "We don't know. The lights went out suddenly, and then we found Noah unconscious on the floor. Something's not right."

"Someone call 911. Get security up here."

Another scream caused a cold fear to clinch the back of his neck. He ran back to the elevator where he'd left Britt, but she was gone. He lurched toward the nursery and stumbled to a stop.

Various hospital employees, including an unarmed security guard, stood in a semicircle around Britt, cradling a baby against her shoulder.

A man stood beside her, a gun to her head.

"Anyone make a move, this woman dies. Let us by, and I take woman out and let her go."

Alexei's nostrils flared. *Yeah, right.*

Alexei shoved his hand in his jacket pocket and caressed his gun as he moved silently toward the reception desk. He didn't want the man to see him with a weapon. If he did, he'd shoot Britt and take the baby. He might even do that now, but he probably didn't want to cause panic among the hospital workers.

Better to walk Britt out of here with the baby, kill her later and take Tatyana's baby—and then kill the baby to destroy all evidence of Olav Belkin's disgusting crime.

As Alexei edged around the reception desk, he met Britt's eyes.

She immediately removed one hand from the baby's back and twirled her hair around her finger. The signal they'd established earlier.

Little late for that. He knew she was in trouble.

When she released her hair, she flicked her hand out to her left side. Then she tipped her head in the same direction.

Alexei's gaze tracked to her left. He swept past a doctor, an orderly and a new mother still in her hospital gown. Then he backtracked to the old orderly and his heart slammed against his chest.

Olav Belkin himself, making sure his baby daughter wouldn't incriminate him.

Alexei had him.

If he took the shot now, who could blame him? Alexei could say he saw Belkin's weapon. He must have one on him. He figured him as a risk to the hospital workers and the baby. DNA tests would soon determine he was the father of Tatyana's baby. Alexei would be exonerated for killing Belkin.

Alexei shuffled behind the reception desk. His eye twitched. A muscle at the corner of his mouth jumped. He pulled out his gun.

Then his gaze shifted back to Britt, snuggling that baby against her chest.

If he took the shot and killed Belkin, the man holding Britt would take his shot and kill Britt...or the baby.

If he didn't take the shot, he'd allow Olav Belkin to defy death again. His crime family would cease to exist—for a while. He'd wind up incarcerated with three hots and a cot and the ability to run his empire from a prison cell.

Alexei raised his weapon and took the shot.

Britt screamed again as the man holding her at gunpoint crumpled beside her.

Epilogue

Britt tucked Summer into her bassinet and smoothed back a soft lock of blond hair from the baby's forehead. "Sweet dreams, *moya solnishka.*"

She curled up in a chair next to the bassinet, tucking one leg beneath her, and grabbed a book.

"Don't you have that baby book memorized by now?" Leanna sauntered from the kitchen, a glass of wine in each hand. "Take this. You need it."

"I'm not the one who was held in a warehouse for over a month getting drugged up."

"I'm not the new mother."

"I'm not either—yet. I'm just the foster mom, and they might not even let me bring her back to North Carolina with me."

"Well, her mother and father are dead, and

I doubt they're going to hand her over to the father's family." Leanna snorted.

Britt sucked in a breath. "You know that Olav Belkin had a heart attack in prison?"

"Of course. Why try to keep it from me?"

"I thought it might…upset you. I mean, remind you."

"I'm not going to forget anytime soon, Britt, but that was the best news I've had in a while. That, and my friend Calvin's going to be okay—back on the street, but okay."

"When are you going to get that tattoo removed?"

Leanna shrugged. "What's one more? Maybe I can have my guy turn it into something cool."

"I wish Tatyana had never confided in you."

"Well, she did, and I confided in Jerome." Leanna sniffed and held the back of her hand to her nose. "How were we supposed to know?"

"I'm sorry about Jerome…and Mila. All that for a little baby."

Leanna reached into the bassinet and traced her fingertip around the edge of Summer's ear. "What did you call her? Something Russian? I think I've heard enough of that language to last me a lifetime."

"It means…" A knock at Leanna's apartment door stopped Britt, and she pressed a hand to her heart.

"It's over, Britt." Leanna patted her knee. "Thanks to you. See what I mean about those nerves? Drink up."

Leanna crossed the room to the front door and peered out the peephole. "Someone to see you."

"Me?" Britt half rose from the chair.

Leanna swung open the door and said, "Hey, navy SEAL guy. Took you long enough."

Britt fell back in the chair. "Alexei."

He stepped inside the small apartment, filling the room with his presence. Filling her heart.

"How's…the baby?"

"She's great." Britt took a gulp of wine.

"Did you two hear the news about Belkin?"

Leanna raised her wineglass. "That's why we're celebrating. Want some?"

"No, thanks."

Sighing, Leanna grabbed the wine bottle by the neck. "If you two don't mind, I'm gonna polish this off in the privacy of my own room."

Alexei leaned over the bassinet and wiggled his finger beneath Summer's chin. "She's a cutie."

"D-did you get all debriefed and everything?"

"I did."

"Was Ariel upset you never made the Vlad connection?"

He lifted a shoulder. "No. I did stop the deal. Vlad will never get his hands on those weapons. After Belkin's arrest, his associates scattered far and wide, and Stepan is cooperating with the authorities for immunity. And the FBI was able to free those women, including your sister and Jessie. That's a win for everyone."

"You didn't get to kill Belkin."

"But I got to save you instead." He perched on the arm of her chair. "A much better deal."

"Did you come here to tell me about Belkin? Are you leaving soon?"

"Yes, yes and yes."

She held up her hand, counting off three fingers. "That's three answers to two questions."

"I answered the third question you didn't ask."

"Who said I had a third question, Russki?"

"Do you want me to ask it for you?" He slid his fingers through her hair.

She rested her head against his arm. "Enlighten me."

"Or maybe I should ask you."

"By all means." Her pulse had started

throbbing in her throat, and her body tingled in anticipation.

"Do you want to wait for me? I promise I'll come back to you—every time."

She swallowed hard. "You're not just talking about this one deployment?"

Alexei slid into the chair, pulling her into his lap. "I'm talking about forever because I can't live without my sunshine."

When he kissed her mouth and ran his hands through her hair, she believed him.

She broke away from the kiss and cupped his jaw with one hand. "You want me to wait for you even though I'll have Summer, the daughter of your enemy?"

"It's not Summer's fault, and that may be just what I need."

"To help me take care of Belkin's daughter?"

Alexei turned his head to press his lips against her palm. "To replace hate with love... because I've discovered that's the best revenge of all."

* * * * *

Look for the next book in Carol Ericson's
RED, WHITE AND BUILT *miniseries,*
BULLETPROOF SEAL,
available next month.

And don't miss the previous titles in the
RED, WHITE AND BUILT *series:*

LOCKED, LOADED AND SEALED
ALPHA BRAVO SEAL
BULLSEYE: SEAL
POINT BLANK SEAL

Available now from Harlequin Intrigue!

Get 2 Free Books,
Plus 2 Free Gifts—
just for trying the Reader Service!

HARLEQUIN *Presents*